John Treherne, Presiden
bridge, is also the author
Paul Theroux described in
tale of mystery', *The Stran*
and one previous novel, *T*

THE TRAP

'A little gem . . . I read this evocative, beautifully imagined novel at a sitting, loving every word of it. It is full of feeling and the haunting power of memory, and conjures up rural English life between the wars with great sensitivity.'
Susan Hill, *Good Housekeeping*

'A recreation of childhood in the manner of *The Go-Between*. He has a lovely sense of countryside . . . a ramble into the fear of a child.'
Andrew Sinclair, *The Times*

'Starts with the air of some highbrow whodunnit of the 1930s . . . Then comes a brilliant intrusion of retrospective violence.'
Norman Shrapnel, *Guardian*

'Extremely accomplished . . . so exact that some of its observations are almost creepy.'
Isabel Quigly, *Financial Times*

'Childhood is a writer's minefield but John Treherne crosses it marvellously well . . . moving, satisfying and good.'
Grace Ingoldby, *New Statesman*

By the same author

The Galapagos Affair
The Strange History of Bonnie and Clyde
The Trap

JOHN TREHERNE

Mangrove Chronicle

GRAFTON BOOKS
A Division of the Collins Publishing Group

LONDON GLASGOW
TORONTO SYDNEY AUCKLAND

Grafton Books
A Division of the Collins Publishing Group
8 Grafton Street, London W1X 3LA

Published by Grafton Books 1987

First published in Great Britain by
Jonathan Cape Ltd 1986

Copyright © John Treherne 1986

ISBN 0-586-07268-3

Printed and bound in Great Britain by
Collins, Glasgow

Set in Times

To William,
my companion on many an island

1

I was distracted from my *Croûte Ivanhoe* by an urgent
tugging at my gown. It had been an exhausting day, a last
bout of hectic shopping three days before Christmas. But
at least I always enjoyed the Fellows' Christmas Dinner.
The panelling of the Hall shone darkly in the candlelight;
the College portraits were decorated with sprigs of holly;
and the Founder's Cup was full of the traditional pow-
dered oak leaves brought that morning from one of the
College farms at Bradenstoke. Oakley was talking to me
but I was barely listening.

Fox, sitting on my left, had been trying to attract my
attention throughout the meal; I had avoided his eye. I
knew that he was still cross with me about the new carpet
in the Fellows' Parlour. There had been three of us on
the carpet committee and I had sided with Appledean-
Stewart in selecting the dark Afghan rather than the
Kiamuri favoured by the odious Fox. Not that I cared
one way or the other about the carpet, but Fox had been
so supercilious that I had naturally cast my vote with
Appledean-Stewart.

To my surprise, it was not about carpets that Fox
wished to harry me.

'As you know, I am tutor to your history undergraduates,' he said, leaning back and sipping delicately at his
claret. 'I refer specifically to De Freville . . . umm . . . A
very able young man.'

He tilted his chair to what I hoped was a dangerous
angle and glared up at the seventeenth-century plaster

7

ceiling. The candlelight reflected softly on the dark hairs sprouting thickly from his nostrils. He cleared his throat and continued with frequent pauses and swallowings which caused his Adam's apple to move alarmingly.

'He is concerned that he is not abreast of the, as it were, latest developments in historical thought.'

This was unexpected. As far as I was concerned, De Freville was far too well informed already. Hardly a week went by without his badgering me about my lectures, my supervisions, my essay topics. Our dispute, early in the term, about the origins of Lollardy was well known in the College; it was even parodied obscurely in the undergraduate magazine and had become a source of considerable embarrassment to me.

I was furious with Fox. He was so massively bland, with the philosopher's usual large contempt for the trivial concerns of a historical specialist. He droned on about what he pretended to think were the problems of this dreadful undergraduate. Smiling amiably, I tried to look as if I did not mind.

Only the week before, De Freville had knocked on my door, ostensibly to clear up a few historical points before going down for the Christmas vacation. I had been cutting my toe nails with paper scissors. At that time of the morning I very reasonably supposed the knock to be that of one of the porters with my mail and hastily hobbled to the door, intending to keep my left foot out of sight as I took the letters. Before I could reach the door it opened to reveal De Freville's long intelligent face. With his soft droopy nose and receding chin he looked very like a camel. He took in my predicament at a glance and insinuated himself into the room, smiling slyly and launching into Bastard Feudalism. He maintained that I had

8

said it was a degeneration from the classic social organization of the high Middle Ages. I suppose I must have done. He had thought a lot about it, he said, and wondered if we could have a talk about it – in depth. What he really meant was that I was quite wrong: modern revision emphasized social stability and the maintenance of law and order. He started quoting recent papers by historians much younger than myself.

De Freville was hell on a cold morning. I hit back as well as I could, suggesting that these men were poor scholars with disabling personal problems, but it is difficult to develop a cogent argument at nine o'clock in the morning lacking a shoe and a sock.

Fox mentioned this incident (or the version of it that De Freville's friends had put about) as an example of his pupil's high motivation. He was afraid such off-hand treatment would dampen De Freville's historical enthusiasm. I wished that I could do a lot more than just dampen De Freville.

I half-listened while Fox droned on about the brilliant promise of his pupil, and then about his plans for Christmas with his old mother in Dorking. I had always been fascinated by his unctuous voice and his dark, spiky eyebrows, which dominated his features like two rows of cypresses on a furrowed cliff face. His shifting grey eyes, underhung by half-circles of sagging skin, regarded me with detached amusement. I realized that he was now talking about me.

'I gather Oakley may be whisking you off to the South Seas in the summer?'

So that's what Oakley had been about to tell me. I guessed that Fox had used the latest De Freville episode as a diversion as well as an irritant. Now he could tease me with his superior knowledge while Oakley was monopolized by the Senior Tutor.

'Yes, I think that he was getting round to telling me when . . .'

'Oh, so you haven't really heard about it yet?'

He damned well knew that I hadn't.

'Hardly your line of country, Yeo. After all – not much call for medievalists in those parts. But still, you are keen on birds and there must be plenty in the South Pacific.'

Fox sipped at his claret, his Adam's apple undulating dramatically.

'Actually, it was my idea for Oakley to take you along to Manabau. It might give you, as it were, a new lease of life.'

It was not until we strolled back to his room for brandy and coffee that I was able to extract anything from Oakley about this expedition. It seemed like a miracle, on a dismal December night – the prospect of the South Seas. The cold penetrated the thin soles of my patent leather shoes, Molly's present last Christmas. I realized that I had never been further south than the Loire or west of Land's End. Molly and I had often wrangled about this, but the car was on its last legs. I had never really wanted to replace the Marina with a dented, showroom reject with that irritating talk-back instrument panel. But it was a knockdown price for a 1983 Austin Maestro and there was no possibility of a new Citroën BX with Molly absolutely determined on getting an antique Spanish garden seat. We couldn't even afford a package holiday in Corfu and there was little chance of travel grants for historians – even successful ones.

Despite the intervention of the detestable Fox, I was flattered that Oakley should want to take me with him to

Manabau, but, as he explained, I was a damned good ornithologist. 'An amateur, in the best sense of the word,' he yawned, as we lolled in the draughty elegance of Oakley's panelled, late-seventeenth-century room which he had recently enlivened with a large poster of Louis Armstrong. 'You know more about Bar-tailed Godwits and the like than any of us so-called professionals,' he continued in his patronizing way.

I had maintained a childhood interest in ornithology and in recent years had published more on the birds of the Lincolnshire marshes than on subjects I was paid to teach. In fact my studies on the Wool Trade in Cricklade, 1536 to 1546, had made no progress at all for at least a year. My room was littered with untouched notebooks, unopened monographs and half-finished manuscripts.

I later discovered that Oakley had approached several card-carrying biologists before inviting me to go with him to Manabau; they had all refused. I didn't mind at all; I was thrilled at the prospect of visiting a South Sea island.

Oakley said that he intended taking along a couple of suitable undergraduates to help him with the research and the daily chores. He would have no trouble finding them. His own pupils would queue up for such an opportunity, he assured me with an embarrassed smile.

That was about as much as I could get out of Oakley. It had been a hectic day, he had drunk far too much claret, he would be sleeping in College. Things were difficult with his wife, he explained.

As I left, I passed Doris Lakowski on the staircase. She had told me that she would be staying up to do some work. Things were not too good back home, she said.

'And how long will you be in Manabau?' That was Molly's first question, when I told her of Oakley's invitation.

11

'And how much will it cost?' She turned away from me in bed. 'And what am I supposed to do while you are away?' She turned off the bedside light. 'And what use will you be on a scientific expedition?'

I could answer none of her questions, but I lay in the darkness full of claret and contentment, determined that I would go to Manabau.

I arrived in College an hour later than usual on the following morning. It was bitterly cold and foggy with a fine dusting of snow on the grass in Old Court. Before going to my room I stopped at N Staircase and clattered up the stone steps to Oakley's room. I opened his outer door and tapped on the white-painted inner one. There was no answer. I looked at my watch – it was ten o'clock. I supposed that Oakley had gone to his laboratory, but banged again to make sure. Then I heard a scuffling noise on the other side of the door.

'If it's the mail, leave it outside.' Oakley's voice was husky and strangely agitated.

'It's me, James Yeo. I'd like to talk to you about Manabau.'

There was no immediate response, only more scuffling. I could hear what sounded like a sofa being moved. After a few seconds, there were some movements closer to the other side of the door.

'I'll come over to your room later, James. Things are in a bit of a mess here now. I'll come over.'

It was odd. Oakley had drunk less than I had at the Feast and was always disconcertingly brisk in the morning, conveying a purposeful importance which I found demoralizing.

I picked up the appropriate volume of the encyclopaedia from the library on the way and took it to my room (I wasn't supposed to do this but my old adversary, Mrs Keating, the librarian, was away with the flu). I'd never heard of Manabau, but I didn't want Oakley to know that.

My eyes drifted down the single column on Manabau:

A group of islands in the south-west Pacific, lat. 174° 30' and 22° 10' S, also known as the Tranquil Islands. Their geology is not well known. The climate is warm with prevailing winds from the east or south-east with occasional hurricanes. Despite statements to the contrary, the inhabitants are the most easterly of the Melanesian peoples. The majority are nominally Methodists, but still turn to the old gods and traditional practices when prayers to the Christian God are unanswered. The islands were sighted by Tasman in 1643 and by Bligh in 1789. Representatives of the London Missionary Society landed in 1800, but were killed by cannibals two years later . . . relapsed into anarchy following the civil wars of 1848 . . . the first governor, Sir Bertram Fildes, arrived in 1877, quelled revolt in the eastern islands and established the administrative capital at Manau . . .

J. R. Moulding,*Geography and History of Manabau (1952).*

I skipped my way to the end of the article, huddled over the gas-fire which had barely thawed the overnight chill in my dank room.

Oakley bustled in at half-past ten. He had shaved, his gingery moustache bristled confidently and his hair was damp and neatly combed. His freckly face was reddened with the cold and he rubbed his pudgy hands together briskly as he picked his way between the piles of books which I had been trying to rearrange on my shelves since the end of term. I made him a cup of instant coffee and we both hunched over the sputtering fire.

I was itching to discover the purpose of Oakley's jaunt to the South Pacific. As far as I could make out he was a laboratory type and the subject of his research inappropriate for desert islands. I had been overwhelmed at the racks of electronic equipment in his laboratory – mysterious flashing lights, oscilloscopes and goodness knows what else. Oakley was, I gathered, the leading international authority on the insect rectum. He had explained to me on more than one occasion that this humble organ concealed some of Nature's most elusive secrets – very important ones, according to Oakley. It had already earned him two doctorates, a silver medal and would, he had once hinted, yield much higher honours in the fullness of time, provided that he could keep ahead of his American competitors who, it appeared, were legion and totally unscrupulous.

It seemed that some insects hold world records for rectal water pumping. If enough locust rectums were laid out flat, to cover a cricket pitch, they would, Oakley calculated, secrete enough water in three hours to float an Amazon Class frigate.

Well, it turned out that Oakley had read a scientific paper which described some extraordinary goings-on in an obscure group of virtually flightless flies. These were found only in the Manabau archipelago. To cope with temporary water shortages these extraordinary little creatures stuck their bottoms into any convenient moist crevice and by vigorous muscular contractions could squeeze the damp air into liquid and then mop it up. It was the mopping-up that interested Oakley. There were several species of these flies, all of the genus *Apterodipteron*. Some stuck their rears into flowers, others into cracks in rocks and one (*Apterodipteron analohydroabsorbis* Erzinclioglu) into iguana nostrils. It was absolutely fascinating, Oakley said. Each island had evolved a different strategy. If Darwin had sailed into the Manabau archipelago, instead of fossicking around in the Galapagos, understanding of Natural Selection would have been much easier, Oakley assured me.

He became so enthusiastic about the scientific aims of the trip that it took me some time to get round to more mundane matters. I was particularly worried about the cost, especially my air fare. There could be severe troubles in that direction with Molly, who would certainly countermand any expenditure on overseas travel that did not include her.

Oakley dismissed my anxieties. Had I never heard of travel grants? He had collected nearly five thousand pounds from two learned societies and a gullible industrial company which was developing desalinating plants for Saudi Arabia. The company was very interested in the commercial potential of his work, he said. I had a fleeting vision of an Amazon Class frigate floating among the palm trees in a shimmering haze. The only travel grant I had ever obtained was twelve pounds eighteen shillings and sixpence, to cover the costs of a visit to Cricklade in 1967. This was small potatoes to Oakley, who didn't think much even of five thousand pounds: it would barely pay for the return flight to Manabau and we had to live there and hire a boat to get around the islands. However, he knew of a bucket-shop in Ealing where we could get cheap air fares. This might leave a few hundred pounds for our expenses in Manabau.

I did not see Oakley again until well after Christmas. Term was in the offing and we had little time to discuss the Manabau venture. Not, as I began to realize, that there was much to talk about, for Oakley was interested in the Tranquil Islands only as a repository of insects with curious habits. *I* was excited at the prospect of balmy, palm-fringed shores, coral reefs and blue lagoons. I took to reading, and rereading, Conrad, Stevenson and Grimble as well as J. R. Moulding's tedious work. I pored over Philip Hartlaub's *Birds of Manabau*. There

15

were, apparently, only about sixty indigenous species in the islands and the Wandering Whistling Duck was now extinct, but there was the exciting prospect of lories, mynahs, lorikeets and megapodes. What is more, I would see them in virtually unspoiled conditions, for, as I learned from February's *Country Life*, tourism was in its infancy in Manabau and was purposely confined to a single island – the greater part of which was a national nature reserve.

Oakley was surprisingly off-hand about the whole affair. I could not even discover which undergraduates were coming with us. His attitude was disappointing. I would have enjoyed making lists, haggling over airline tickets, poring over maps, accumulating equipment. As it was, we would hardly have any equipment and had not even booked our tickets.

Oakley became increasingly withdrawn and preoccupied as the term dragged on. I hardly saw him. He lunched only occasionally in College and rarely dined. We sat next to one another at the February Governing Body meeting, but even then he virtually ignored me and pored over the typed drafts of one or other of his innumerable scientific papers with his head cocked ostentatiously to one side as if to advertise his ability simultaneously to push back the frontiers of rectal science and to keep up with the tortuous wranglings of the assembled Fellowship in the gloom of the Large Combination Room.

It was at the March meeting that Oakley hinted at what was troubling him.

'I've got a hacker in my net – I'm sure of it.'

'Really? A hacker, eh?' I did not want to sound stupid, for in his present troubled state I knew that it would annoy Oakley. To have a hacker in your net sounded fairly rustic, like having a ferret up your drain-pipe. I guessed that he was having trouble in the garden – his only interest apart from the locust rectum.

'Somehow, he's got into Janet. I don't know how, but I'll fix the bastard, don't you worry.'

Further communication was prevented by the arrival of the Master, who could just be made out in the half-light at the far end of the room executing his usual prancing bow to the Senior Fellow. I was so stunned by Oakley's remark that I was unable to concentrate on the protracted discussion which followed. It concerned the proposal to issue female undergraduates with a booklet (to be approved by the Chaplain) on contraceptive practice. Clearly Oakley's troubles were not horticultural. I had never been introduced to his wife, although I had seen her, dumpy and rather cross-looking, shopping in Sainsbury's with Oakley on Saturday mornings. Whoever this Hacker was, he seemed from Oakley's typically coarse phraseology to be on the most intimate terms with Janet Oakley. Perhaps that was why Oakley had slept in his room after the Fellows' Christmas Dinner.

The argument by this time had moved on to the colour of the roses in Old Court, and as the College medieval historian I was expected to have important views on this. The Senior Fellow maintained that the roses should be white, for the House of York. After all, he argued in a quavering, barely audible monotone, Hugh Blunsden had lived in Old Court. As a 22-year-old Fellow of the College he had rallied to the forlorn Yorkist cause by leading a handful of undergraduates in support of Lambert Simnel at the battle of Stoke in 1487. But the matter was far from straightforward; the despicable Fox (who had clearly boned up on the matter to put me out of countenance) broke in and 'reminded' the meeting that the Founder

17

himself was related ('distantly and, as it were, improbably, but nevertheless, I emphasize to the Fellowship, *related*') to Katherine Swynford who, I had forgotten, had married the third son of John of Gaunt. According to his view, which I afterwards realized was quite wrong, the roses should be red, for the House of Lancaster. Fortunately, my fatuous suggestion that we should plant pink ones was persuasively supported by Simms (the morose Reader in Agricultural Ergonomics, and the only academic I knew who answered to the name of Reg), and to my surprise this was carried by an overwhelming majority.

The candles were lit at four o'clock and I had the pleasure of seeing quite clearly that the Master was executing a series of curious bobbing movements in my direction – to signal, I assumed, his gratitude for my solution to the problem of the Old Court rosebed. Cecil Fox was revealed to be white with fury at my success, but I could barely relish the pleasure of this unexpected victory. Poor Oakley's awful predicament might threaten our expedition to Manabau.

Oakley made no attempt to enter into the deliberations at that dreadful meeting. Despite his membership of the external finance committee, he remained silent during the discussion that followed the Master's announcement of a hundred and fifty thousand pound benefaction which had been offered to the College. The anonymous benefactor had stipulated that the money should be made available for the use of visiting graduates from Kramer College, New Jersey, while they were in the United Kingdom.

The main difficulty was that no one had heard of Kramer College although the name seemed vaguely familiar to me. The Senior Tutor was adamant that we should not accept the benefaction. In his view, it would confer

18

no direct financial benefit on the College and very little academic distinction. On the other hand, the Bursar (a cheerful Devonian of miserly instincts) was impressed by a subsidiary clause, namely: the provision of a further five thousand pounds *per annum* to enable a recently qualified College lawyer to spend an unspecified period at Kramer College. Preference was to be given to a chancery practitioner.

Oakley left the meeting during the discussion of this item, which was eventually deferred to the July meeting, and I missed the chance to corner him when we drank the customary white port in the Small Combination Room.

It was later, when I was hurrying back to my room in a thin drizzle, that I recalled where I had heard that name before. Doris Lakowski was from Kramer College. She had seemed embarrassed when telling me about it during her College interview. According to Doris there was much ill-informed gossip and racial prejudice against Kramer College in certain quarters in the United States. Still, there was no doubt about Doris's intellectual calibre. She was a bright girl, rather too plump, with a rasping voice, dark intelligent eyes and long black hair. The trouble was that she devoted so little of her energy to history, and even then in a most idiosyncratic way. Doris was always 'into' things. There was no doubt about what the things were, for they were emblazoned on her T-shirts which faithfully recorded her ever-changing interests. On her arrival, I recall, it was women's liberation: this phase involved the preservation of under-arm hair, which she absentmindedly groomed in supervision classes, the renunciation of deodorants and an unrestrained, lightly-clad, bosom printed with the words 'Feminism is Fun' and 'Women Need Men Like Fish Need Bicycles'. Then there was her Greenpeace period ('Save Dwarf Gibbons' and 'Stop Bloody Whaling'), her flirtation with the Hare Krishna sect (a time of abstract motifs) and her current obsession with self-sufficiency and alternative technology ('Small's a Ball' or 'Do It Yourself It's Fun That Way').

It never occurred to me to wonder why Doris had abandoned her studies at Kramer College. I was just grateful to have her among my undergraduates – not least because she so frequently drove De Freville mad during supervisions with unorthodox historical notions invariably coloured by her latest obsession (he was particularly incensed by her representation of Bess of Hardwick as a prototype for Germaine Greer). Doris had the additional advantage of being a thorn in the flesh of her tutor, Cecil Fox, whose worst fears concerning the admission of women into the College she amply confirmed. Typically, however, his attitude to his pupil underwent a dramatic change after he had met the extravagantly rich Lakowski Senior during his memorable visit to the College at the end of the Lent term.

It was about this time that Oakley's affairs reached crisis point. I had been watching him carefully for some weeks, worrying that the expedition would never take place. One morning I went to the length of visiting him in the shabby maze of rooms where he conducted his research into the locust rectum. I had to discover whether the expedition was still on.

It was a cloudless morning in early April, but I found a tousled, shirt-sleeved Oakley sitting in a stuffy cardboard cubicle staring at the screen of a computer terminal. I knew that he was proud of this device, which, he had boasted to me in College, was somehow linked to other computers and could consequently perform all sorts of electronic marvels.

20

However, the marvels that it had been performing that morning were not at all to Oakley's liking.

'Look at that!' he bawled. 'Look at that! It's done it again.'

He gestured wildly towards the faintly glowing screen which bore the words: 'BIG BROOOTHER IS WATCHING YOU.'

'Is that so terrible?' I asked nervously. 'It's probably just something wrong with your program or a hiccup in the computer, or perhaps someone's playing a trick.'

'I'll say they're playing a trick,' he squeaked. 'Whoever it is has got into my files and must know everything that's in them – that's all!'

He spun round and rummaged along a shelf, pulling down what looked like the soft-covered volume of a symposium proceedings. He shuffled among the pages and then stabbed a pudgy, neatly-manicured finger at an article half-way through the book. From the running title I could see that it had been written by Oakley and one of his research students or other collaborators.

'That's a nice thing to find in a respectable scientific paper, isn't it?'

I peered at the offending lines. They certainly dealt with the subject of Oakley's research but in an unexpectedly obscene way and in a far from scientific context.

I must admit I was shocked.

'You didn't write that, did you, Oakley?'

'No, of course I bloody didn't,' he snarled, his normally pale skin flushed between the freckles. 'That's the whole point. Someone doctored the damned disk before we sent it off for electronic printing in Hamburg. Because it was on disk there was no possibility of error and five thousand copies were run off and sent out to all the delegates at the Bratislava meeting.'

'But didn't you check the proofs?' I asked nervously. 'We always do with the *Wessex Historical Review*.'

'You don't need to check proofs with this electronic publishing. They've got to be the same as my print-out. Someone may have glanced at them in Bratislava, I suppose, and a fat lot of good that did.'

Oakley was sitting slumped in his stainless-steel executive chair holding his head. His hair was dishevelled and his moustache drooped dejectedly.

'My whole bloody career will be in ruins if it goes on like this,' he groaned. 'I suspect that bastard Titheridge in Baltimore. It's just the sort of dirty trick he would pull after I took him apart in last year's *Advances in Insect Physiology*.'

I was now completely mystified.

'But how could anyone in Baltimore mess up your computer terminal?'

'Because the computers are linked, damn it! And that means that *all* my data could be doctored, for all I know.'

There was little one could say in the circumstances. The way things were going I could see I had a fat chance of getting to Manabau.

2

I was deeply depressed after my meeting with Oakley in his laboratory. Not only were there Oakley's marriage difficulties and the sabotaging of his computer, there was also the fact that he had made absolutely no arrangements for our South Sea islands trip.

Molly was marvellous at this time. She had come to realize just how much the expedition meant to me and did everything she could to help and distract me. She even offered to type the manuscript of my paper on the Cricklade wool trade, which was unfortunately still incomplete, and on at least two occasions she actually suggested visits to the Lincolnshire saltmarshes and the north Norfolk coast, where there was wonderful bird-watching to be had.

I appreciated her concern and felt closer to her than I had for many years, but as things turned out my worries were entirely unfounded.

I realized this in an instant on a damp May morning when I spotted Oakley walking with Cecil Fox between scattered crocuses across the newly cut grass in Old Court. He was transformed. His surly, harassed expression had gone and he made no attempt to avoid me, as he had been doing for several weeks. As they passed, he paused in his conversation with Fox, and called out:

'Everything's all right now – I've sorted out the computer business. We must be thinking about the Manabau thing fairly soon.'

His voice had acquired an unfamiliar lightness of tone.

I was so moved that I was unable to reply. I noticed Fox regarding me, his spiky eyebrows raised in sardonic amusement.

Oakley patted my arm encouragingly. I think that only at that moment did he realize how much I wanted to go to the South Pacific. He squeezed my arm as we parted and lowered his voice.

'It was nothing to do with Janet after all.'

I was delighted, but dared not speak of such a personal matter in front of the grinning Fox. However, I was determined to let Oakley know just how happy I was at the turn of events.

The opportunity came in unexpected circumstances the next day, a Saturday. I was shopping in Sainsbury's with Molly and we were enjoying ourselves deciding what sort of groceries I might find in Manabau.

It was then that I spotted Oakley wheeling a trolley laden with tins of dog food and packets of breakfast cereal past a pyramid of baked-bean tins. He was wearing jeans and a pale blue anorak. His wife was at his side. They looked cheerful, almost as though they too were sharing the excitement Molly and I felt. I was so intoxicated by all these unexpected feelings that I rushed across to Oakley and grasped him by the hand. He looked surprised, but I didn't care.

'Glad you've patched things up with Janet,' I said and then, looking straight at Mrs Oakley, blurted out, 'Marvellous to see you both together again.'

I returned to Molly feeling better than I had for a long time. She was looking puzzled.

'What on earth did you say to them?' she whispered. 'They're looking at you in a very odd way.'

But I did not look back, for I was heading for the wine

section where I had spotted some bottles of Spumante that were much cheaper than those in the College cellars.

Oakley was waiting for me when I arrived at my room in College on the following Monday morning. He was leaning against the door and I could see at a glance that some of his troubles had returned.

To my surprise, he barred the way to my door and stood, gingery and belligerent, directly in my path.

'What the hell did you think you were talking about in the supermarket on Saturday?' he demanded. 'Have you gone off your head or what?'

I was so taken aback that I could only stammer in surprise.

Oakley continued. 'If it's any satisfaction to you, my wife has not spoken to me all weekend and I'm sleeping in College *again*.' He paused, took a step towards me and growled, 'Why were you jabbering about patching things up with Janet? Who in hell is Janet?'

'Isn't your wife Janet?'

'No, she's Muriel,' Oakley bawled, 'Muriel bloody Oakley and is unlikely to be so for much longer if you have anything to do with it!'

'But I'm certain that you called her Janet and said that she was . . . well . . . going with this Hacker person.'

Oakley glared at me for some seconds in disbelief.

'Janet, for your information – you oaf – is short for Joint Academic Network. It's a computer network! A hacker is someone who breaks into a network – any network – JANET or TELECOM GOLD or TELENET. The hacker in this case turned out to be the despicable Trevor Michley, the research student I kicked out last year. He now has, or I should say had, a job in the Computer Lab.'

With that, Oakley turned and waddled away. He had an expressive, rather conceited bottom which now also conveyed outrage.

It took some days to re-establish my relationship with Oakley. When I approached him in the quad that evening he told me to piss off. Two days later he cut me dead outside the Porter's Lodge and the day after that nearly ran me over with his Datsun as I was walking across the Fellows' car park.

Improbably, it was Cecil Fox who brought about our reconciliation. He must have enjoyed the whole thing enormously and particularly relished extracting from Oakley the details of my idiotic part in the proceedings. Nevertheless, for once, he did a kindly thing: it was almost as though he was anxious for me to go to Manabau. Not that I felt at all kindly disposed to Fox, for it was he, I was convinced, who had recently spread about the College that extremely childish nickname for me, 'Yo-Yo' ('he's always going up and down his string') Yeo, which now seemed to be in general currency among the undergraduates.

Fox's strategy seemed to involve several long visits to Oakley's house in Hillingdon Drive to placate Muriel Oakley – and, I have no doubt, to explain away the whole business in terms of my incipient insanity. Having convinced her of this, it was apparently quite easy to bring Oakley round. To give him his due, Cecil Fox was quite tactful. The first I knew of his intervention was a note in his neat, miniature script, suggesting that I should take sherry in his (Fox's) room on the following evening. I would most probably not have accepted his invitation but for the concluding, heavily underlined sentence ('*Please come, it will be greatly to your advantage to do so*'). It was intriguing, although, as I was fully aware, it could be some sort of vulpine joke.

Cecil Fox was at his most affable that evening. Oakley had already arrived when I stumbled up H Staircase in almost total darkness (the light bulb had blown) and burst into the comfortable grandeur of Fox's elegant blue and grey rooms. Fox was showing Oakley some newly-acquired baubles for his ivory collection – statuettes of Napoleon Bonaparte and Voltaire. It was an embarrassing moment, but Fox did not falter. His manner was as smooth and mellow as the brimming glass of sherry he handed me. He came straight to the point.

'It is . . . um . . . singularly satisfying for me to bring together again, as it were, two such valued colleagues.' Fox's epiglottis was working at full capacity. 'I feel almost part of your expedition – to which, I know, James, you are particularly looking forward.'

Oakley, I noticed, even from the depths of my embarrassment, was looking stunned. It dawned on me that he must have had no idea of the extent of Fox's interference in his affairs when he accepted the invitation to sherry.

'I gather from Oakley here that the final arrangements are not, as it were, in hand,' the ass droned on. 'If I can be of *any* help then please regard me as being entirely at your disposal – for whatever purpose you may, as it were, regard as expedient.'

Fox now behaved like a pompous housemaster trying to buck up a pair of ineffective sixth formers who were in danger of messing up the school outing. I would not have been surprised if he had invited Oakley and me to put the gloves on in the gym and then to shake hands. I could not imagine what he was up to. Yet perhaps he was cleverer than I gave him credit for at the time, because

27

his absurd behaviour led Oakley and me to bolt, together, as soon as was decently possible.

'Now don't forget – anything I can do to help,' Fox called as we groped our way down the unlit staircase. The unctuous insincerity of his voice was more than I could bear.

Outside, the College lamps glowed faintly in fading sunset light. Oakley paused briefly before going back to his room.

'Well, at least he talked Muriel round.'

Two days later events took another alarming turn when Molly called to me through the bathroom door that Muriel Oakley was on the telephone. I was feeling particularly ragged that evening. I had not mentioned to Molly the contretemps with Oakley, and there had been yet another nerve-racking encounter that afternoon with De Freville, who had pretended to be thirsting for detailed knowledge of medieval land tenure. Molly had got very angry earlier in the evening about the dinner party with Aubrey and Hilary Doncaster for which, according to her, we were already very late. To make matters worse the car was playing up and I had just cut myself shaving while trying to snarl back at Molly's insistent urging to 'hurry up, for God's sake'.

The prospect of conversation with Muriel Oakley was the last straw. The awful realization struck me of what Cecil Fox might have said to her in his oily, carefully-contrived tones ('Is that the sort of man that you would . . . um . . . trust on a desert island with your husband, Mrs Oakley? Just think what he might do if real danger, as it were, threatened . . .'). I could imagine him taking one of her stubby hands into his smooth soft ones and gazing into her close-set eyes.

'Hello, Mrs Oakley. How nice of you to telephone.'

She answered with what seemed like a suppressed sneeze.

'Mrs Oakley?' I repeated.

'Yes, it's me, Dr Yeo.' It dawned on me that she had been laughing.

'That's nice . . .'

'I thought that I really should telephone to thank you for making possible my unexpected trans-atlantic jaunt.' She laughed openly after this. Her voice was infectious and warm. How different she was on the telephone.

'How do you mean – trans-atlantic jaunt?' I asked lamely.

'With Derek, of course,' she giggled. 'I just felt like letting you know. You see, if there hadn't been that mix-up in Sainsbury's I would not be going to the States.'

'America . . . ?'

'Yes, California – Pasadena, actually. Derek is leaving tomorrow for a Workshop in Baltimore on – well – you know what Derek works on, I suppose?' She laughed again. 'And I'm flying out next week to join him in Pasadena, where he's going to do some work with Zak Titheridge. Derek is particularly fond of Zak.'

'I'm glad, Mrs . . .'

'You can call me Muriel, James. I'd like that.'

'Yes, thank you, but how on earth . . . ?'

I was forced to break off by a sharp jab in the kidneys delivered at short range by Molly.

'James? Are you still there?' Muriel sounded genuinely alarmed at the prospect of a breakdown in communication.

'Yes, I'm here. It's just that we have to be off soon to dinner.'

'So I'd better come to the point. Well, there are two

things really. First, to thank you for mixing me up with Janet. You see I gave Derek such a bad time that the poor man offered to take me with him to the States – a thing that he has never done before. I also shamelessly recruited your friend Cecil Fox. He worked wonders with Derek. And the second thing is to give you a message from Derek. There will hardly be any time when we get back from the States, what with examinations and all, to contact you before you leave for Manabau.'

'Yes?' I was fascinated by her voice, compelling and seductive.

'So, Derek, who is running about like the proverbial pea on a drum, has asked me to telephone you to say that his secretary will buy the tickets and leave yours in College. You will see the departure time from Heathrow on the travel agency envelope. Derek says to make sure that you've had your injections and that your passport is OK. Just bring tropical gear in a rucksack. Derek gave you a list, I believe. He will bring scientific equipment and the rest is to be loaned by a laboratory in Manabau. I will be driving Derek to the airport and you could come along as well if you liked. There will be plenty of room in the Datsun.'

'Yes, that would be very nice. Thank you.'

I felt another sharp jab in the lumbar region.

'So that's that . . . Muriel Oakley faltered. She seemed almost reluctant to finish our conversation.

'Just one other thing,' I babbled as the tattoo on my back increased. 'Who else is coming?'

'Oh, some of Derek's students. I don't know who they are. He never tells me things like that.'

'Muriel?' I gasped, desperately trying to prolong the conversation.

'Yes, James?'

'If there's anything I can do before *you* leave . . . please let me know.'

There was a gentle peal of silvery laughter and a click – followed by two sharp blows in the small of my back.

I have alway been susceptible to the warmth of a woman's voice and Muriel Oakley's attracted me. Clear, but softly modulated, it conjured up the image of a fair lady with a high intelligent forehead and wide-apart eyes; tall, with a humorous mouth. It seemed entirely disjoined from the dumpy woman with close-set eyes I had seen in Sainsbury's.

I tried, unsuccessfully, to telephone Oakley twice before he left for Baltimore. Muriel answered on both occasions and each time I was transfixed by her honeyed tones. We gossiped inconsequentially on random topics while Molly was, on one occasion, in the bath and, on the other, making a crêpe Suzette.

Muriel had told me when she was to drive Oakley to Heathrow. It was therefore with some surprise, when I answered the telephone in College that same afternoon, that I heard Muriel Oakley speaking. There were one or two things we should clear up, she said. Could I pop round to Hillingdon Drive?

'When would be convenient?'

'How about *now*?' she replied. 'Actually, I'm feeling a bit low after seeing Derek off and could do with some company. Why don't you come to tea?'

So it was that I headed for number 27 Hillingdon Drive at 5.32 precisely, on an unexpectedly sultry May afternoon. I parked the car opposite number 25 (the Oakley's Datsun had been left in the road outside their house) and trotted, self-consciously, in blossom-scented sunshine past neatly-trimmed privet and a larch-lap fence towards an oaken gate, redolent of linseed and bearing an oval, poker-worked sign: 'Oakleigh'.

The sign rather unnerved me, but I opened the gate, scrunched along a neat, petunia-lined gravel path and activated Oakley's 'Big Ben' door chimes.

The door seemed to fly open almost immediately.

'It's nice of you to look in, James,' Muriel giggled. Only her head showed round the half-opened door, which also seemed to have been anointed with linseed. 'I was just freshening up after the drive. Come in, come in. I'll pour you something.'

She waved me into a cool, white hall. Here all was lavender polish and an unseasonable smell of hyacinths. A half-finished painting of Oakley in scarlet doctor's robes was leaning against a reproduction Tudor blanket chest.

Muriel Oakley regarded me with detached amusement. She was leaning against the closed front door, her close-set eyes twinkling; her stubby fingers clutched a purple kimono (a present from Oakley's visit to Japan, the previous year, I guessed) which had parted to reveal the disconcerting whiteness of a chubby leg, marbled with the blueness of tiny veins radiating from a massive central delta just below the knee.

'I thought I'd better come in . . . in case you . . .' I stuttered. 'In case' of *what*, I was now beginning to wonder.

'Yes, I thought you might, James.'

I was disconcerted by her amused certainty, by the overpowering respectability of lavender polish and hyacinths and could only gape at the awful reality of Muriel Oakley. Her face had a sort of menacing fish-like quality, like a piranha seen head-on. Only her eyes seemed human. How could I have been so affected by her disembodied voice? More important, how in hell could I get away from what I felt might well turn into a difficult situation?

Muriel sensed my confusion, and may have understood its cause. But she knew what she was about (from considerable previous experience, I guessed) and led me firmly but very gently by the arm, into a spacious, sunlit sitting-room. I was conscious of bluebells and of silver-framed photographs of Muriel and Oakley artfully deployed on a gleaming grand piano. There was a bright-ly-polished brass coal scuttle beside a flower-filled hearth. A dog was barking somewhere at the back of the house.

'Well, what's it to be?'

Muriel stood looking down at me, her eyes still twink-ling in her oval fishy face, as I perched on the edge of a tasselled Parker Knoll sofa, shifting a carefully placed copy of *Country Life* from beneath my right buttock.

'How do you mean?' I croaked. She seemed surprised by my uncertainty. I sensed that she had a very clear idea of what 'it' might be. I repeated my question in an extremity of apprehension.

'Drinks. What do you want to drink, you silly man?'

'Um . . . I thought we were going to have tea.'

'No, no. Not *now*. So what's it to be? Sherry? White port? A Dry Martini? Sweet Cinzano? Or would you like some of Derek's Glenfiddich?'

'Oh, that . . . please,' was all I could manage in reply.

I was beyond rational decision and picked up the bent copy of *Country Life* to examine minutely the advertisement for a recently restored Tudor manor house in the Cotswolds (offers in the region of £350,000).

A heavy, cut-glass tumbler was thrust into my hand. I swished the contents into a straw-coloured whirlpool and stared at it, hypnotized and frantic. Muriel deftly flicked

33

shut the apple-green velvet curtains across the leaded french windows, shutting out the late afternoon sunlight. I could not pretend not to notice this.

' Does Molly know you're here?' she said.

Her voice rose and fell in the exquisitely beautiful cadences which had caressed my inner ear on the telephone.

'It is Molly, isn't it?'

I ignored the question. Muriel refilled my glass. Of course Molly did not know where I was. How could she? Muriel had only telephoned half an hour before.

She was now sitting at my side, her hand momentarily *brushing my knee*, talking and talking in the pungent bluebell-scented half-light. I could not take in more than one word in ten. I felt like a rabbit with a stoat.

'You're not so cocksure as Derek.'

I gulped and choked on a mouthful of Oakley's whisky.

In the gloom Muriel thought I was laughing and giggled in a silvery trilling manner which made my hair stand on end.

'You're not – well, not in the way I meant.' She laughed again more hesitantly. 'Derek is dreadfully *direct*. Life is so simple for him. He goes for what he wants – and he usually gets it.'

This was horrifying. And there was that word 'it' again. Good God, I remember thinking, this is dreadful. I just had to get away from this appalling woman. I drained the glass in a single reckless swallow and felt as if the back of my throat was burning out. Speechless and dizzy with the whisky, I dared not to move and Muriel had *again* brushed my knee with her hand.

What followed is painful to recall. What's more, it is rather difficult to remember accurately, for Muriel's cut-glass whisky tumbler was even larger than I had thought.

However, I remember becoming conscious of the ticking of a carriage clock, which seemed unaccountably loud. Muriel's kimono had slipped to reveal the nursery slopes of a surprisingly mountainous and startling white bosom.

I gaped in admiration and panic.

Muriel seemed only at this point to have realized the extent of my agitation. Her face went quite pink; her whole attitude changed. She pulled the kimono tightly across her chest and looked strange and haughty.

I felt an odd wave of gratitude to her now that I knew I was safe. After all, she had been about to offer herself to me, and to be desired even by an ardent piranha was an extreme sort of compliment. Her failure to evoke an answering passion must have been a blow to her pride, and indeed she was now looking pretty cross. I was moved to something like pity and tried to pat her on the arm. It was all I could think of. I felt so sorry for her. Muriel appeared to leap to attention and instead of stroking her arm in reassurance I found myself pushing drunkenly at the front of her kimono.

She jumped to her feet and glared down at me, her fishy features distorted with anger.

'I think you had better leave, James,' she said.

She stalked out of the room and I could hear her fiddling with the front door latch. Then she called to me from the entrance hall.

I struggled to my feet and blundered into the dazzling sunlit hall feeling as if I had been flamed in alcohol. Muriel was standing belligerently by the open front door.

I felt some words of comfort would be appropriate. After all, we were both civilized human beings. I was especially sorry that I had wounded her by my feeble lack of response, but it really was all for the best.

35

I tried to explain this, but she simply closed the door in my face.

I left 'Oakleigh' just after six o'clock. I must admit that I was very anxious about the whole episode. What on earth could I tell Molly? Even worse, there was the danger that Muriel might regale Oakley with some garbled version of the encounter on his Parker Knoll. From her abrupt change of manner, I knew she had been very put out and might well represent the whole thing as an attempted seduction on my part – either from spite or in an attempt to cover her tracks in case I should ever blow the gaff to Oakley.

I had difficulty starting the Maestro and chugged off unevenly down Hillingdon Drive, my head throbbing, trying unsuccessfully to devise a convincing explanation for the car having been parked outside Oakley's house. I had just remembered that one of Molly's pals at her oil-painting classes – a horrible, inquisitive, painted woman called Margery Rodford – lived somewhere in Hillingdon Drive.

I was desperately relieved when the day passed for Muriel Oakley to leave for Pasadena. Not unexpectedly, there had been no further telephone calls to or from number 27 Hillingdon Drive. I had frequent nightmares in which I was pursued by an enormous fish with white mammary glands, but I cheered up considerably as the early summer days lengthened and term came to an end in a welter of examinations and interminable examiners' meetings. The only snag was the curious behaviour of De Freville. The imminence of the examinations seemed to have sapped some of his confidence, but none of his maddening persistence. There was a nasty moment when he returned to the subject of Bastard Feudalism and a worse one when we got on to the painful topic about which he had nagged me earlier in the year: the effects of the Black Death on late medieval heresy. Now I had devised this subject for an essay, partly tongue in cheek, in a vain attempt to put him in his place. I reckoned it would keep him occupied and, if he did by chance come up with any ideas on this subject then, I could, after an interval, use them as the basis for a short article in the *Historical Review*.

Unfortunately, my strategy proved quite wrong. De Freville went for me root and branch. He had thought long and hard about the subject, he said, and as far as he could see there were *absolutely* no effects of the Black Death on the growth of heresy in late medieval England. Could I provide him with a few suggestions? Perhaps there were some review articles he had overlooked? Did I know of some unpublished work which had not come to his notice? He went on and on, until I was forced to send him away.

As finals approached, however, De Freville became extremely anxious and began to have doubts. His baroque mind told him that I might have known more than I had revealed about the Black Death. The whole concept was so improbable that there could just be some underlying truth. Perhaps in the recent shake-up of the examination procedure (in which he took an intense and unhealthy interest) there might be some sort of novel, non-regurgitative examination technique. Was this the case, he demanded? If not, why on earth had I proposed the topic in the first place? Did I know more than I had revealed at the time? Well, I was not a man to kick an undergraduate when he was down, but I could not resist the opportunity of keeping De Freville there. I implied that some very stimulating changes were certainly being considered in the examination procedure, that my whole motive in setting that essay topic had been to test his critical faculties.

The effect on De Freville was satisfying. It was the first time I had had the upper hand. His whole attitude changed and he listened to me quite respectfully in the last two supervisions of the term while we went over his previous essay topics and he rabbited on about a recently published series of articles on the origins of the Peasants' Revolt which I had failed to spot.

The time passed pleasantly while I made all the preparations for the jaunt to Manabau. However, my peace of mind was rudely shattered. Molly broke the news to me when I returned home on a warm evening with swifts hawking and screaming in the clear air.

'The wife of that friend of yours rang – the one who is taking you to those islands,' Molly called from the kitchen and then switched on the liquidizer.

My bowels heaved. Was Muriel trying to cover up her own part in the affair on the sofa or extract revenge by shifting the blame in some way?

What had she said to Molly?

'Is she all right?' Molly shouted over the whirring of her machine.

'Eh?'

'I *said* is she all right?' Molly bawled back.

'What do you mean *all right*?'

'It's her voice. Quite extraordinary.'

'They say in College that her voice is the best thing about her.'

'I'd hate to think what she looks like if that's the case,' my wife bellowed.

'You've seen her, actually.'

'I have?'

'Yes, that time in Sainsbury's when . . .'

'Oh, *that* woman. Good gracious.'

'Well, what did she want?'

'She seemed quite huffy. Said she wouldn't be able to drive you to Heathrow. Have you upset her about anything?'

'Er . . . what did you say?'

'*Have you upset her about anything?*'

'No, no. What did you say to *her*?'

'That I'd take you. She will have a lot to do with getting her husband's things together. They've only just got back from the States, apparently. She's going to speak to you about something at the airport, she said.'

Molly switched off the liquidizer. It moaned with a discouraged note and stopped.

3

Molly drove me in thin drizzle to Heathrow. We planned to get there early, to breakfast together before the Oakleys arrived. I had left a note for Oakley saying that I would meet him with the others in the departure lounge at half-past ten: at least that way I might avoid Muriel, although there still remained the anxiety of the first meeting with Oakley since that embarrassing encounter with his wife. I shudder to think what she might have told him. Curiously, I began to experience feelings of guilt.

Breakfast was a disappointment. We arrived late, the restaurant was crowded and Molly spent ages in the loo. There was only time for coffee and a stale croissant before hurrying to the departure gate and a clumsy farewell from Molly. She looked so tired.

Oakley was waiting for me at the entrance to the departure lounge, buffeted by a tide of noisy Norwegian teenagers and plainly flustered.

'Where the hell have you been?' he squeaked, pushing me into a fat Indian lady in his agitation. 'They've been boarding for ages – the others have gone on.'

Oakley propelled me along endless corridors and moving staircases, past electronic gadgets and bossy officials. Everywhere was a faint, sickly smell of aviation fuel. A disagreeable air hostess jammed me into a seat next to a dark-haired young man wearing a purple shirt open to his navel. To my relief, Oakley was deposited somewhere in front of me.

It took me some minutes to recover my composure in

the over-heated atmosphere. Fortunately I was at the end of a row and, after a few more minutes, began to take stock of the other passengers. They seemed to be mostly young men, rather flamboyant in a common sort of way, with a sprinkling of elaborately coiffured women. I was overwhelmed by the scent of after-shave and perfume.

During the take-off I contrived unconcern, attempting to read the copy of *The Times* which I had found on the seat. The great aircraft climbed through billowing clouds into brilliant sunlight. I thought of Muriel Oakley and of poor Molly, thousands of feet below, ploughing their separate ways back along the M4 in sunless gloom towards their empty homes. I began to relax – the first time for weeks – and ordered a Martini from an amiable middle-aged hostess. Even the stirrings of guilt about Muriel Oakley subsided. I resumed inspection of the other passengers and opened the complimentary bag of roasted peanuts.

It was then that I noticed the ear, two rows in front of me: a large, prominent right ear with a pimple on the lobe. I could recognize that ear anywhere. What of earth was De Freville doing on board?

Before I could recover from the shock of recognition a grinning young woman with long dark hair and a turned-up nose rose from her seat next to the owner of the ear and looked back. It was Doris Lakowski.

Doris smiled, clambered out into the aisle and walked to my seat to crouch on her ankles at my side. She was clearly amused at my surprise.

'Doris. I didn't know you were coming.'

She smiled again.

'And what in the hell is De Freville doing here?'

'Now take it easy. All will be revealed in LA.' Doris

put her hand on mine, as though pacifying an excited child.

'It was Dr Fox's flash of genius,' she grinned. 'Anyway I need the can . . .' And that was as much as I could extract from Ms Lakowski.

'You her Dad, then?' my purple-shirted neighbour addressed me from the other side. I opened and then shut my mouth.

'Well, are you? Her Dad, I mean?'

I replied after a great effort at self-control.

'No, she's American. I'm her supervisor actually.'

'Not bad. Not bad at all. How many chairs do you have then?'

'Chairs?'

'Yeah, chairs. Things you sit in – C-H-A-I-R-S.'

'Oh, chairs.'

'Yeah. How many?'

I decided to humour the man and made a quick mental count: starting with the dining room, then the parlour, before adding in the ones in the kitchen and bedrooms. After some effort I was able to answer.

'Twenty-six.'

'Jeez . . . you must have a big place.' He poked a companion in the row in front. 'Guy here has twenty-six chairs.'

'Some operation . . .' came the reply.

'Yes,' I agreed, quickly re-opening *The Times*.

I noticed that Oakley was holding court with three young men, one of whom was wearing a pale-blue jump suit. De Freville was deep in conversation with a tall blonde, resplendent in bandeau and ostrich feathers. I decided to experiment with the 'in flight entertainment'.

Oakley strolled up as I was struggling unsuccessfully to plug in the plastic ear-phone set which I had hired at exorbitant cost. I mustered what I knew was going to be a sickening placatory smile. Oakley was relaxed and in good humour. Our fellow passengers were delegates to an international hairdressers' convention in Los Angeles, he explained. They were good fun. The one in blue was called Julian, he continued, but his voice was drowned by loud guffaws from his new-found friends in which I distinctly heard the phrase 'Amazon Class Frigate'.

'Silly oafs,' Oakley snarled and turned abruptly away.

Guilty or not, this was my opportunity to get out of him why he, and evidently the meddling Fox, had plotted to Shanghai *me* with De Freville on a tropical island. I cornered Oakley at the rear of the aircraft. He was gazing down at the distant slate-grey ocean through the window of an emergency exit.

'I know what you're going to say,' he mumbled apologetically, 'but it's not like you think. My own undergraduates let me down . . . It was Cecil Fox who suggested De Freville.'

So Fox had got his revenge. I waited with very mixed feelings for Oakley to continue as he flattened himself against a bulkhead to avoid the returning drinks trolley.

'You see, De Freville's great-grandfather discovered a species of petrel in Manabau. It's not been seen for years and De Freville wants to find out if it's still around. He's keen on birds apparently, and Fox thought that it would be a good opportunity for you and De Freville to make it up.' Oakley sipped at a tomato juice and regarded me apprehensively.

'But why didn't you tell me what was happening?'

'Well, that's the whole point. Fox thought that you wouldn't go if you knew that De Freville was going. It was his idea that you should become reconciled. De Freville is very well liked in the College. Fox is convinced

43

that he has the makings of a brilliant scholar . . . it . . . it rather reflects on you if this feud goes on for another year . . .' Oakley faltered into silence, crushed his empty plastic cup and resumed his examination of the North Atlantic.

I was trapped and there was nothing that I could do about it. Damn Fox *and* De Freville. I quailed at the prospect of weeks of protracted historical wrangling about Lollardy and Bastard Feudalism, as De Freville harried me with his contorted historical arguments. And there would be Doris to witness my humiliations. As if I did not have enough to worry about trying to look Oakley straight in the eye and not think of his fish-faced wife sprawling on their Parker Knoll, her breasts bulging out of her kimono.

What was Doris doing here anyway? That was the other thing I wanted to straighten out with Oakley. Three historians on a biological expedition – it was ridiculous.

Oakley was evasive about the unexpected addition of my favourite undergraduate to the party. He reached out to pour more tomato juice into a fresh plastic cup, helped himself to a packet of peanuts and peered gloomily through the window before answering my question.

'It was difficult. My students weren't as enthusiastic as I had expected. The chance to take Doris came up at the last minute . . . her room is on my staircase, you know.'

'But Doris wouldn't know a Swamphen from a bull's foot. And why the devil did you keep it all so quiet?'

'That was part of Fox's plan after he'd talked to the Master, and then me, about De Freville. If we'd told you about her she might have blurted out that De Freville was coming. We told her that it was going to be a surprise – you always said that she was your favourite undergraduate.'

That at least was true, although I couldn't imagine Cecil Fox wanting to give me a pleasant surprise. Although no great beauty, Doris could look quite pretty on one of her good days and I sometimes discreetly flirted with her when the opportunity presented itself. It was difficult to believe that she was actually on board and I remember looking down the lines of close-packed seats for a glimpse of her dark hair.

I was interrupted by the arrival of Julian and his pals, *en route* for the toilets and more tomato juice for the Bloody Marys that they were concocting from their duty-free bottles of vodka. Julian attempted to embrace Oakley, saying that they shared some common interests.

'Very common indeed, if you ask me,' shouted one of Julian's entourage.

Oakley fled.

'Twenty-six,' Julian addressed me with intoxicated respect. 'Adrian says you have twenty-six chairs.'

I smiled non-committally.

'And taking along that nice little brunette to LA. I wouldn't mind supervising her . . .' He dug me in the ribs as he lurched towards the nearest lavatory, which had just been vacated by my purple-shirted neighbour, who, I deduced, must be Adrian.

I followed Adrian as he shoved his way between excited knots of delegates and was surprised to find my seat occupied by Oakley, deeply engrossed in my copy of *The Times*. He looked up apologetically.

'Hope you don't mind swapping seats, old boy. It's a bit awkward for me over there.'

There was little that I could do, short of making a scene. I moved on with a sinking heart. The prospect of De Freville was infinitely more daunting than the close proximity of the objectionable Julian and his colleagues.

45

De Freville rose as I approached and stepped into the aisle. We shook hands. It was an awkward moment, but I handled it admirably.

'Well, De Freville, what's it to be? Bastard Feudalism or . . . ?'

'Nothing like that I hope. I was rather looking forward to a chat about birds.'

I found it difficult to imagine De Freville engaging in such a cosy mode of communication. Doris winked at me as I squeezed into Oakley's seat, to sit between my two undergraduates.

'Bet you never thought you'd be bopping off to the South Pacific with us two,' she giggled.

Despite my apprehensions, I felt a very agreeable sense of companionship – and, at least, had avoided my near-cuckolded colleague. I even managed a cheerful nod to Julian whenever his head appeared over the back of the seat.

What would have been unbelievable even five minutes before happened: De Freville and I chatted amicably throughout lunch *and* while Doris was watching a movie about some unattractive American teenagers. We did not speak of Lollardy or the origins of the Peasants' Revolt. Our talk was of wading birds and breeding plumage, of migrations, territories and flycatchers. De Freville was clearly a competent field ornithologist. He lacked experience, but more than made up for that with his enthusiasm.

De Freville told me that it had been his ambition since childhood to rediscover the petrel that bore his name, *Pterodroma defrevillei*: a small dark-brown bird, it had been first described by his great-grandfather, Sir Humphrey De Freville, when he had been Governor of Manabau. It apparently nested only on a few islands in the archipelago and had not been recorded since 1894.

His grandfather had searched for it when he too had been Governor of the islands just before the war, but without success.

I must have fallen asleep while De Freville was telling me about his petrel, for the next thing I remember was being shaken by Doris and having a plastic tea-tray thrust in front of me. Doris said that my head had been resting on De Freville's shoulder.

4

De Freville's head was on *my* shoulder when I glimpsed the first of the outlying Manabau islands. The plane was low enough to see waves breaking on a fringe of coral, the grey shape of a huge fish in the pale turquoise waters behind a barrier reef, dark-green mangroves, then tree-clad mountain slopes veiled with coiling mist, the deep blue of a lagoon and, once more, open sea.

The others were still dozing. We were dishevelled, jet-lagged and dog-tired.

The plane flew on through wispy clouds. Below appeared further coral reefs, more sea, another island and then a muddy river winding through dense green forest and, here and there, grassy clearings with clusters of bamboo huts and upturned canoes.

We hurtled towards a verdant mountainside, then turned and dropped between two low wooded hills to land with a series of stomach-shaking jolts on a runway cut into the red soil of a forest plateau. The plane bumped its way on rock-strewn gravel towards a single-storey concrete building, streaked with rust from rooftop railings. A large notice announced, 'WELCOME TO MANAU INTERNATIONAL AIRPORT'. The roof was jammed with people. A military band, in scarlet tunics and grass skirts, was drawn up in front of the terminal building.

There were only about a score of passengers on the Air Manabau plane which had flown us from Fiji. Most of them were Manabauans. Their plump black faces were wreathed in smiles. They exuded boisterous good humour

48

as they picked up their parcels and banana-leaf bundles. It was their commotion as much as the jolting of the landing which awoke my companions. The excitement increased as the door was opened, but subsided abruptly when a khaki-clad police officer entered. He swept his way into the cabin with an imperious wave of his cane and spoke to the air hostess. They both glanced in our direction.

I felt uneasy. It would be just my luck to be turned back now on some administrative technicality. I was fishing for my passport, visa and work permit in some agitation when the hostess beckoned to Oakley. He too looked nervous. Fortunately, the police officer left as the hostess spoke to my companion.

After a few moments, Oakley turned and fairly skipped down the aisle.

'It seems they've laid on an offical reception,' he explained as he helped Doris lift down her travel bag. 'They evidently want me to go first. I had no idea that my work would amount to anything here.' He was clearly delighted at the prospect of this moment of glory. I was pleased for him too – it somehow made up for that silly mix-up on the sofa with Muriel – and despite his faults he was a well-meaning chap who, after all, had worked extremely hard at his research.

The other passengers stood aside as Oakley strode to the opened door, followed by Doris and then De Freville and me. Oakley paused to wave to the rooftop crowd. At the bottom of the steps stood a rotund gentleman, resplendent in a white uniform, with scarlet sash and ostrich-feathered hat.

Oakley hesitated as he approached the grand person-age. I guessed that he had just realized his ignorance of protocol. After all, an Englishman likes to do the right thing, especially on ceremonial occasions. However, Oakley could never have predicted the greeting that he received.

'Mr De Freville, this is indeed a great pleasure.'

Oakley stood with his mouth open, then closed it and gulped before replying.

'I'm Oakley, actually – Dr Oakley. De Freville is an undergraduate, the pupil of my colleague Dr Yeo. I must say that I am very honoured . . .'

'You mean that you are *not* Mr De Freville?'

'Well . . . Yes, that is, no . . .' Oakley was forced to admit.

'Then please stand aside. There seems to have been a mistake.'

The khaki-clad policeman stepped forward, grasped Oakley's left arm and propelled him to one side.

'Then where *is* Mr De Freville?' the welcoming grandee demanded.

'Excuse me, Doris,' De Freville muttered and tripped down the last four steps to occupy the space so abruptly vacated by poor Oakley.

'My name is De Freville, sir.'

The rotund gentleman beamed and offered a large black hand to my undergraduate. There was tumultuous applause from the rooftop and a deafening blast of sound as the grass-skirted band commenced a spirited rendering of what I assumed was the Manabau National Anthem. In the shadow of a wing I could see the policeman waving his cane threateningly under Oakley's nose.

It took Doris and me some time to get into the airport terminal. Our progress had been barred by four large, rather jolly-looking policemen who kept us standing in the overpowering heat on the steps until the welcoming party, De Freville and the military band had departed.

There was no sign of Oakley. Doris and I sat, tired and dispirited, on an uncomfortable wooden seat as the scruffy airport building gradually emptied.

'Just wait till I catch up with that creep,' Doris grumbled. 'I'm beginning to see why he got your back up, Doc.'

It was the first time that Doris had adopted that annoying form of address, which made me sound like one of the seven dwarfs. However, at least it was better than 'Yo-Yo', and I felt considerable sympathy for her attitude, despite my recent, probably short-lived, reconciliation with De Freville. After all, the wretch had abandoned us without a backward glance and, at that very moment, was no doubt being lavishly entertained. His grandfather must have been a very big noise in Manabau.

It then occurred to me that I had no idea where we were supposed to be staying in Manau. Oakley had arranged all that, but, for all we knew, he was being charged with high treason at that very moment.

'Mitmee,' Doris replied.

'Mitmee?'

'Yeah. It's probably some stupid acronym, but it's where we *were* going to stay in this dump.'

There was a tattered map of Manau and district pinned to the wall and I spent some minutes in a futile search for our destination.

Oakley appeared while I was still looking. He was surprisingly cheerful and seemed not the least cast down by his recent humiliation. He said that his captor had been at Uppingham, Oakley's school, and, what was more, was thinking of sending his son to the College. The police officer had arranged for us to be taken down into Manau.

The Manabau Institute of Terrestrial and Marine Ecology turned out to be a collection of rusty Nissen huts scattered among tall palms at the western end of Manau Bay. The guest house was a long thatched bungalow with a wide veranda, set in a grassy clearing amidst scarlet-flowering frangipani bushes, close to a sweeping sandy beach, gleaming white in brilliant sunshine. Waiting for us on the veranda was a cheerful-looking Manabauan matron. She was clad in a length of multi-coloured cloth, wrapped tightly around her ample frame, and was clearly in a state of considerable excitement.

'You must be the friends of Mr De Freville,' she called to us in perfect English as we tottered towards the veranda steps in an advanced state of fatigue and heat stroke.

'This is indeed a great honour – I never expected to meet anyone who knew Mr De Freville,' she chattered on. 'My sister-in-law has just returned from the airport. She said that Mr De Freville looked just like she expected a young English lord would be.'

I could hear Doris muttering away behind me about what she would do when she caught up with the 'lousy creep'. Oakley was silent. It was left for me to mount the rickety veranda steps, grasp a large friendly hand and blurt out a hastily-contrived greeting.

We followed our hostess along the veranda into a long gloomy room, shuttered against the tropic heat. There was a pleasant smell of cooking. A large jug, flanked by three glasses, stood on a bare, scrubbed table. We slumped into canvas chairs, surrounded by our discarded baggage, and gratefully gulped the cool passion-fruit juice offered to us by our genial hostess.

In no time at all Rua had covered the table with a large yellow cloth and laid out a delicious meal of fish cooked in coconut milk, a bowl of steaming mutton stew and a pile of exotic fruit.

We took our coffee on to the veranda. The shadows lengthened and we watched our first Manabauan sunset with the palm trees etched in black against the vast crimson sky. We were all very tired but Oakley insisted that we should make plans for the next day. He would go across to the Institute to get together the equipment and see about the boat which we were to be lent, while Doris and I would go down into Manau to buy food supplies for the expedition. We avoided any reference to De Freville, for we were still annoyed by his defection and had no idea when he would reappear.

Despite the fatigues of our journey I awoke early the next morning. Rua was already clattering about and talking to Oakley in the kitchen. There was a continuous chirruping of a bird close to my shuttered window – I longed to know its species.

We took breakfast on the veranda. The air was pleasantly warm. Palm leaves rustled high overhead and I could hear the regular thump of the waves on the beach. Oakley was in exuberant mood. Somehow, he had become surprisingly friendly with Rua. The two of them laughed and giggled, quite unnecessarily, each time that she appeared bearing, successively, newly-baked bread rolls, a large jug of milk, bananas, cups of excellent strong coffee, more rolls and then fresh coffee. Rua was clearly fascinated by Oakley's ginger hair and ruffled it with her pudgy fingers every time she passed close to him. I found it *very* embarrassing. Surprisingly, I could see that Doris was not pleased either. She looked tired and hardly ate any breakfast.

Rua's passing interest in Oakley's hair paled to insignificance beside her major obsession. There was ample evidence of it on every inside wall. Three decades of royal history were enshrined there, from faded, fly-blown magazine photographs of family scenes on the lawns at Balmoral in the early 1950s to glossy colour photographs of Princess Diana in picture hats.

We soon discovered that Rua had an encyclopaedic knowledge of British royalty. She could identify the most obscure progeny of lesser royal Dukes. But none evoked the same degree of enthusiasm as did De Freville.

The shopping excursion with Doris was great fun. As Rua had instructed, we stopped and boarded the ramshackle lorry which appeared to be the only form of public transport into the centre of Manau. Doris had recovered from her breakfast-time depression and we sat together on rough plank seats, clutching at the tattered canvas awning and our seemingly more stable fellow passengers, as the ancient, blue-painted vehicle rattled along a rutted, palm-fringed road at the apex of a billowing cloud of red dust. From our lurching platform we saw palm and scrubland give way to mangroves, mudflats and then a sea wall, revealing a harbour view. A tree-lined boulevard led from the harbour. Doris poked my arm and blew a raspberry at the street sign – De Freville Avenue.

Our first port of call was the Army, Colonial and Planters' Emporium in Frith Street. Rua had directed us there and we had no difficulty in finding it – a tall wooden building, white-painted and ornate, shuttered against the mid-morning heat. In its gloomy interior we discovered a long mahogany counter with many elaborate brass fittings and two huge, slowly-rotating ceiling fans, The staff, who appeared to be exclusively Indian, were white-clad and obsequious, but managed to induce in me at least strong feelings of social inferiority.

Fortunately, Doris was not overawed by the late-Victorian splendours of the Army, Colonial and Planters' Emporium and briskly set about a vast grocery order. Each item was carried from the stacked mahogany shelves and placed reverently on the polished counter for our inspection and approval. Everything that we purchased was redolent of the days of Empire, from the twiddly black designs on the labels of the jam jars to the tins of corned beef decorated with a lion and crossed Union Jacks, and blocks of Lifebuoy soap which were exactly as I remembered them as a child, and they had seemed old-fashioned even then. We bought two huge tins of what looked like ship's biscuits and a sack of flour, bags of oatmeal, sugar, rice and raisins, jars of Marmite, tins of curry powder and condensed milk, Earl Grey tea and coffee essence, all pushed into large metal drums with snap-on lids for protection against the ravages of the Manabauan insects, rats and God knows what else.

Doris arranged for the groceries to be delivered to the guest house that afternoon and Rua had undertaken to buy vegetables and fruit for us, so we had the rest of the morning to ourselves.

We bought postcards and stamps and then took coffee at Morgenstern's. I had badly wanted to do this, to wallow in colonial nostalgia among the wickerwork chairs of this plush Edwardian hotel, famous throughout the South Pacific for its literary associations. We walked through the lobby, with its huge brass fans and tall decorated ceiling, on to the terrace for the view of the Manau waterfront.

I noticed the long grey shapes of three anchored warships and a red and white hydrofoil skimming across the smooth water of the harbour.

We sat in the shade of a hibiscus tree and scribbled away at our postcards. I had chosen one for Molly of a group of piccaninnies with a goat. As we left we stopped at the hotel's ornate yellow post-box. Doris hesitated before dropping her cards into the dark interior of that Victorian relic. I noticed that she still held the postcard of a frizzy-haired warrior standing by a war canoe which she had selected for her father. I playfully tweaked it from her hand and pushed it in with Molly's piccaninnies.

Oakley was sitting on the veranda when we returned. He looked cross and waved listlessly. I was still intoxicated with strange feelings of happiness, but was fairly short with him.

'What on earth's the matter? You look as though . . .'

'It's the boat,' Oakley groaned. 'I've never seen anything like it and the other equipment isn't much better, I can tell you.'

'But I thought you had arranged all that?'

'I did, or thought I had,' he squeaked. 'I wrote *three* times and made it *quite* clear that we needed a sea-worthy craft . . .'

It took considerable patience to coax the truth from him. It appeared that there was only one craft available, an ancient clinker-built cabin cruiser, which had been abandoned ten years earlier by a bankrupt Australian chiropodist and presented to the Institute by a generous government. Despite its title, the Manabau Institute of Marine and Terrestrial Ecology had recently terminated its marine programme – hence the availability of the research vessel, *Bounty II*. The name was a bad omen, but it was not that which was upsetting Oakley.

Later in the afternoon we walked over to the muddy creek which served as a dock. *Bounty II* was certainly not what might be expected of a modern scientific research vessel. To me, she looked more like the *African Queen*, an impression which was strengthened by the uncanny resemblance of the black boatman to Humphrey Bogart – peaked cap pushed back on cropped greying hair, hanging cigarette and all. I think it was this that upset Oakley more than anything about *Bounty II*. He clearly had expected an efficient modern research vessel, bristling with expensive equipment and a proper crew.

Personally, I rather liked the look of *Bounty II*. What worried me was the health of the engine and the difficult question of who was going to operate it, for it had slowly begun to dawn on me that black Bogey (whom I had also begun to like) would not be accompanying us on our expedition to the remote islands. It was he, in fact, who finally made it quite clear that we would be alone in the boat. There was no one who could be spared, he explained, and in any case he had to go back to his village to help with his niece's wedding.

Oakley began to bluster about how he could certainly manage 'a properly fitted-out and sea-worthy thirty footer'. It was this particular 'thirty footer' that worried him. Now here he clearly upset Bogey, who was evidently very attached to *Bounty II*.

'I would like you to know, sir,' he announced in perfect English with dignity and emphasis on each word, 'that this here is a very fine boat. She is, of course, not an ocean-going vessel, but for island work she is first class – really *first class*.'

He continued to enumerate the virtues of *Bounty II*, finishing with the admission that her engine could be 'contrary'.

'You've got to handle her like a woman. Then she'll work for you. But you all got degrees and them things so she shouldn't be no trouble. No trouble . . . and besides, it would cost you more than *two hundred* dollars a day to hire a motor boat down at the harbour.'

It did the trick. We did not have that kind of money – and, as far as Oakley was concerned, it was the end of the matter.

'If you think I'm going to risk my life in that damned thing, then you've got another think coming,' he snarled, as soon as Bogey strolled off to resume stacking a huge pile of coconuts which was evidently a prominent feature of the Institute's research programme.

'What are we going to do then?' Doris and I chorused.

'We shall have to work around here, I suppose.'

'Awh, com'on – we can't chicken out *now*,' Doris bawled.

Oakley shook his head and kicked at the dusty ground like a dejected five-year-old whose Christmas present was not up to scratch.

'Come on, Oakley,' I butted in, 'we can't just stick around here. Most of the birds I want to see are out in the islands and there's no chance at all of De Freville finding his petrel in the suburbs of Manau.'

'I tell you I'm not going to carry out my research in a wreck like that. Quite apart from the safety aspect . . . it's . . . well – just not suitable for what I have in mind.'

Oakley stamped his foot petulantly. Bogey stopped stacking coconuts, the better to observe the pantomime: I was concerned that he might hear Oakley's tirade and come over to create an even worse scene about the denigration of precious craft.

What a mess. It was so infuriating: only twenty-four hours on the island and here we were already arguing bitterly, with the prospect of several weeks' confinement on the outskirts of Manau and no sign at all of De Freville. Yet only an hour and a half before I had been sitting happily with Doris on the terrace of Morgenstern's with the glorious prospect of sailing off on the next morning's tide. Blast Oakley *and* De Freville; to hell with both of them.

Then I let fly.

'Now look here, Oakley,' I stormed. 'I'm going out on that boat tomorrow, with or without you *or* bloody De Freville, and you're coming with me, aren't you, Doris?'

She nodded loyally.

'You bet, Doc. I'll be with you as we sail into the wide Pacific.'

With that, Oakley turned away and waddled off in the direction of the bungalow, his bottom juddering conceitedly; Bogey resumed his coconut stacking; Doris winked at me. But I was in deadly earnest. This was my chance for a few glorious weeks of adventure – and I was going to sail amongst those islands if it was the last damned thing I ever did. I had not been so worked up since that embarrassing incident with those yobbos at Cricklade in 1971.

Supper that night was a subdued affair. Doris was now very grumpy. She was cross about Bogey's sexist remarks concerning *Bounty II*'s engine, was still jet-lagged and seemed increasingly upset about De Freville's absence. Oakley sulked about *Bounty II* and it was left to me to gossip, with very mixed feeling, to Rua as she prepared and served our evening meal.

Despite her relaxed manner with Oakley it turned out that, like most Manabauans, Rua was an enthusiastic Methodist. She had been born in a village on one of the larger islands, some seventy-five miles to the west. Her life there had been regulated by the beating of the drum which summoned the worshippers to the little coral church standing at the centre of the village. According to Rua, Methodism had come late to the outer islands, at the turn of the century, just after the unfortunate death of the Reverend Mr Skinner. Many of the old beliefs still survived in the islands, Rua hinted, especially in times of trouble. She could not tell me much about these customs. They were the prerogative of the men of the village, but she knew that, among other things, they had to do with the taking of the sacrament, although Ribena was normally used and was especially imported from England for this purpose. Yet in times of storm, pestilence or other disasters 'the old ways' were invoked and the elders would take off for the sacred isle. This was, apparently, only some twenty miles down the coast. It was, Rua said, a huge flat-topped rock surrounded by mangroves at one end of a much larger wooded island. The isle was so sacred that it had no name, even on official maps and charts.

In the old days, Rua said, couples found in adultery would be taken to the island and ritually stabbed to death by the injured parties. I had the frightening image of Oakley pursuing me with a carving knife and of Molly going at Muriel Oakley with our kitchen cleaver.

I also remember wondering what else still took place on the nameless isle in times of emergency and whether they would meet with the approval of the Methodist Conference.

Rua chattered on to me about the life and customs of her people as Oakley sprawled on the veranda and Doris rested in her room. I was impressed with Rua's knowledge and vocabulary. After all, she was just an ordinary Manabauan woman, but here she was speaking clearly and lucidly in a foreign language. I remember thinking that she would not have disgraced me if I had taken her to dine at the High Table. How would she have got on with Cecil Fox, I wondered?

Rua was clearly very curious about the purpose of our visit. I found it difficult to provide a satisfactory explanation. Really, when viewed objectively, Oakley's research was rather ridiculous and quite embarrassing to explain to non-specialists. Still, I would never have had the chance to come to the South Pacific if it had not been for Oakley's bizarre scientific interests.

As we gossiped, it dawned on me that Rua did not know the identity of, or even that there was, a fourth member of our party. When I told her, she at first disbelieved me. Then she recalled that four people had been booked into the guest bungalow but that one place had been cancelled about a month before by the Director of the Institute.

Far from producing the pleasure that I had expected my revelation to induce, my announcement caused Rua considerable anguish.

'You mean that Mr De Freville might come to stay in *my* guest house?' she gasped. 'Why didn't you tell me before? This is awful.'

Rua spilled the soup on the paraffin stove in her agitation.

61

'But Rua,' I soothed, 'I thought that you were very keen on Mr De Freville?'

'So I am . . . so I am,' Rua moaned, 'but how can he live in a place like this?'

'I think that it is *very* nice indeed here, Rua.'

'So it may be – for you. But for Mr De Freville . . . oh dear.'

I was upset to see our hostess so distressed and continued in my attempts to soothe her, not least because I could see that there was imminent danger of our supper being ruined. I eventually succeeded in calming Rua by convincing her of the improbability that Mr De Freville would ever cross her threshold. *We* would undoubtedly be summoned by him, I argued.

Rua soon recovered her good spirits. She was too optimistic and amiable to be depressed for long. It was then that she told me a curious thing which confirmed for her my theory that she would not be called upon to entertain the distinguished visitor. There had been no sign of Mr De Freville all day. He was supposed to have opened a new infants' school that morning and to have visited the Manau sewerage works in the afternoon. But there had been no sign of him. Rua knew this, because her sister-in-law had waited at the school and outside the sewerage works, and Mr De Freville had definitely not appeared. In Rua's opinion, my pupil had *disappeared*.

I went to bed early that night, at about nine o'clock I suppose. Supper had been a dismal affair, what with Oakley sulking and Doris unusually subdued and grumpy.

Despite my fatigue, I found it difficult to sleep and eventually fished out my well-thumbed copy of Hartlaub to refresh myself on the distribution of flycatchers and warblers in the archipelago. Unfortunately, my bedside paraffin lamp attracted an amazing assortment of insects, including several Stuka-like mosquitoes. It was just as I was about to turn out the lamp that the door opened to reveal Oakley standing there in strawberry-coloured pyjamas.

'I've been thinking about the boat,' he said, kicking at the rug with a bare, knobbly foot. 'I'm not prepared to take the responsibility for putting to sea in that cockleshell, but if you agree to take charge, then . . . well . . . I suppose I'll come along.'

5

We all woke early the next morning. There was so much to do, and I had slept badly. Oakley had made it clear that it was all now my responsibility and I was worried about De Freville. I was more than a little frightened at the prospect of our voyage on *Bounty II* and apprehensive about our chances of survival on a desert island – even if we managed to reach one. I thought, guiltily, of Muriel Oakley and then of Molly: she would have had her supper by then and would probably be watching television all on her own. What on earth had brought me to this pass?

Why hadn't I kept my mouth shut about how I was going to sail off in the *Bounty II*, come hell or high water? Christ, I even found it difficult to cope with the Maestro. I could never manage any mechanical repairs: Molly had had to change the tyre when we had a puncture at Wootton Bassett and always did the map reading. Yet here was Oakley trying to put all the responsibility on *me*. Christ!

Fortunately, my forebodings subsided somewhat with the freshness of another dawn as I struggled for the first time into the khaki drill shorts and bush shirt that Molly had dubbed my 'explorer's outfit'. I had taken a lot of trouble to get shorts of just the right length and was naturally very irritated at Doris's merriment. She said that I looked like a pre-war College basketball player. Even Rua was sniggering in a corner of the kitchen. I was relieved that I had not brought the solar topee which I had been tempted to buy at the army surplus stores near the College.

After breakfast we walked across to the jetty to clean up *Bounty II* in preparation for loading. The vessel looked even more forlorn than it had the day before. It rested lopsidedly on the mud at low tide, surrounded by busy fiddler crabs. A solitary Mangrove Heron was perched on the cabin roof.

It is difficult to sweep and scrub the interior of a tilting boat and we were very tired after a couple of hours at it. But the old craft looked neater inside after we had finished. While Doris and I were carrying over our luggage and stores and collecting camping equipment from the Institute, a strangely subdued Oakley was given a crash course on marine engines by Bogey.

The water started to flood into the creek at about eleven o'clock and by midday the *Bounty II* was afloat, loaded and ready to sail. Rua had walked down to the jetty to witness our departure. Even the Director of the Institute, a fat Samoan in a mauve T-shirt, strolled across to wish Oakley success with his research project.

We had a last-minute palaver about De Freville. I was against leaving without him, but Oakley (who still looked cross) and Doris (who now seemed sad) both insisted that we should sail forthwith. It was his own fault, they argued: I had been right about him all along. He had gone off in his vainglory leaving us to fend for ourselves. Oakley's humiliation at the airport evidently still rankled; Doris's pride had been dented. So, I was out-voted and that was that, but I remember thinking that it would look very bad in the College if it became known that we had abandoned an undergraduate on a South Sea island.

*   *   *

The engine chugged satisfyingly as *Bounty II* nosed her way out of the muddy, mangrove-lined creek into the bay. My early morning fears receded. Ahead of us was a sparkling immensity of turquoise water. The horizon was edged with a thin line of white that marked the outer margin of the barrier reef. To the north there were no breakers and that was where we were to aim to get through the reef and into the open sea.

It was flat calm and baking hot as we churned our way across the huge bay. Oakley was at the wheel in the deckhouse while Doris and I pored over a chart laid on the fo'c'sle decking. Fortunately, our course was clear. Once through the gap in the barrier reef we would head out to sea for half a mile or so and then steer due west ('turn left' as Doris described it) along the coast for Raboa – the third of a dozen or so islands that were strung along the south-western shores of Manabau. Oakley had selected Raboa for our first camp because it was inhabited (there were villages at either end of the island) and because of the particularly fascinating rectal habits of some of its insect inhabitants.

It all seemed surprisingly straightforward and I lay down to relax on the fo'c'sle deck. Doris sat up by my side with her chin on her knees, looking out for submerged reefs and enjoying the passing scene. She was wearing one of the long kaftan dresses which seemed to be her standard apparel for the expedition.

From the changing motion of the boat I felt when we were nearing the open sea and propped myself up on one arm. It was infernally hot. My immediate vision was dominated by the brown and white pattern of Doris's dress. I sat up. The dazzling sea seemed purplish and was everywhere flecked with white; behind us, in the turquoise calm of the bay, was a tiny fishing boat and a motor launch.

The outlet through the reef, which had seemed a mere chink from the shore, was more than two miles wide and *Bounty II* ploughed safely into the rolling Pacific swell. We held to our course until the long line of breakers was well astern and then turned slowly westward, keeping the shore on our port side. As we did so, I noticed that the launch had cleared the reef and was following in our wake. One of two white-clad figures in the bows was waving energetically. There was going to be trouble, I was convinced of that. We had forgotten to inform the customs of our departure or had omitted some other necessary bureaucracy. We could be drug smugglers for all the authorities at Manau Harbour knew.

Oakley looked worried. He slowed the engine and handed me my binoculars. I focused – and there were the grinning features of De Freville. He was waving his arms above his head in some excitement.

It really was too bad of him. I have always had a quite irrational fear of pursuit by uniformed authority. My mother said it was because I had been badly frightened by a friendly policeman who thrust his face too close to my pram. I must admit, I was very rattled by that menacing police launch.

We managed to scramble De Freville and his baggage aboard with some difficulty, for the stationary boats were heaving about alarmingly.

'Where've you been, you crazy bastard?'

'Damn you, Doris,' the prodigal retorted as he waved perfunctorily to the departing police launch, 'I've had a hell of a time I can tell you . . . and what do you mean by leaving without me?'

'*Us* leaving without *you*? Did we screw up your coronation then?'

My two undergraduates sniped at one another for some minutes while Oakley got the boat moving and I stowed De Freville's gear in the cabin.

De Freville was upset by his reception. Between his exchanges of unpleasantries with Doris I managed to piece together what had happened to him after his desertion. He maintained that he had had no option but to fall in with the ceremonial at the airport.

'Anything else would have been too embarrassing,' he explained. 'I had no idea that they were going to do anything on that scale and there seemed to be no point in dragging in the lot of you. It was such a bore . . . what with all that eating and drinking.'

It transpired that De Freville had been whisked from the airport to the Commissioner's Residence where he was accommodated in considerable splendour. There had been a dinner party that night at which, jet-lagged and heavily intoxicated, he had fallen asleep. He had been undressed and put to bed, he learned later, by two hefty matrons. He had overslept the following morning, missing the projected visit to the infants' school, and had refused outright to go to the sewerage works. He had tried to contact two of his college pals, for whom, at Cecil Fox's instigation, he had been instrumental in getting vacation jobs with a tourist agency in Manabau, but learned that they were not working in Manau. That afternoon he had been borne off by some English friends of his family for tea and then a dinner party and, next morning, had overslept again. If it had not been for the intervention of the Commissioner's resourceful secretary he would not have caught up with us.

Poor De Freville. I felt guilty at the black thoughts I

had harboured against him. Doris also relented and gave De Freville a hug. Only Oakley seemed unmoved and continued to glare out from the deckhouse. To give him his due, this may have been because of his difficulty in hearing and concentrating adequately on De Freville's explanations. But I think there was more to it than that. Oakley really had been bitterly disappointed and humiliated in what must have seemed a glorious moment at Manau Airport. Then there had been all that pettiness about the poor old *Bounty II*. I had come to realize that he was embarrassingly ambitious. Perhaps most scientists are. After all, there was that half-finished oil-painting in the hall at 27 Hillingdon Drive and there had to be some very powerful motive for a man to devote his adult life to the study of frog sperm or insect backsides.

Because of Oakley's sulkiness it was left to me to explain our immediate plans to De Freville. As I told him, we had, in Doris's words, already 'turned left' and all we had to do now was count the islands as we passed them and stop at the third.

As I might have expected, my pupil raised a number of niggling doubts, criticisms and complicating factors. He was particularly concerned at the dilapidated state of our antique boat and our lack of nautical experience. Oakley, who was clearly enjoying his new role, scowled anew at De Freville. De Freville grumbled at the absence of navigational aids and was very put out indeed when he discovered that we had not notified the authorities of our intended destination. However, he cheered up when I told him that there was radio equipment on board.

At about two o'clock we saw land ahead, standing well out from the mainland shore which had receded to a faint dark line and then disappeared altogether. I reckoned that we were making excellent time. Despite De Freville's doubts, we were, in fact, managing splendidly. I remember thinking that the average sailor must be, well, pretty average and that a couple of dons (with *three* doctorates between them) should be able to cope with the relatively simple matter of sailing a boat down a few miles of coast to find a large island.

We could see reefs and behind them dark-green mangroves and low wooded hills. I spied my first Wandering Albatross and De Freville spotted some Wedge-tailed Shearwaters skimming over the waves.

The land fell astern and once more the *Bounty II* was nosing across open sea. Ahead was a grey-greenish smudge. Oakley shouted that it must be the second of the islands. The sky was deep blue but there was a large bank of clouds to the south, I assumed over the mainland. Fluttering among the waves was, I am sure, a Gould's Gadfly Petrel. It certainly had rather bluish plumage, but I couldn't see its legs clearly.

We came abreast of some rather nasty-looking coral reefs at about three o'clock. Behind was a lagoon and the inevitable dark-green line of mangroves. It was close to low tide and through the binoculars I could see the spindly feet of those ubiquitous tropic trees sticking, like giant claws, into the wet sand. There was no sign of human activity: not a village, a canoe or a fishing boat. De Freville thought that he heard the distant sound of an aeroplane, but none of the others did.

Oakley was now in excellent spirits, although still not speaking to De Freville. He was convinced that the next landfall would be Raboa.

'Might even get something to eat in one of the villages,' he called out. 'Rua said that if you just turn up, the chief will look after you.'

'Like Highland hospitality?' De Freville interjected.

'Something like that,' Oakley growled.

Well, at least they had communicated. My spirits rose further. It seemed like a marvellous dream after the worries of the early part of the day. I winked at Doris and remembered our morning together in Manau. Life was definitely *not* over at fifty-three.

The astonishing thing was the speed at which *Bounty II* seemed to be travelling. We must have covered more than fifty miles since midday. Oakley said that you couldn't tell at sea, there were tidal flows, winds and ocean currents which made it difficult to estimate the distance travelled.

Well, there was hardly any breeze and I had just seen a floating branch which looked remarkably stationary. I fished out the chart again. There was Manau Bay and, sure enough, the string of islands which included our destination, the third one – Raboa.

It was then that I noticed on the chart the two long fingers of land that ran northwards from the mainland. Could we have mistaken those for the first two islands? If we had, then it would certainly explain our improbable speed.

I proposed my theory.

'Balls,' Oakley shouted, unnecessarily.

I persisted. After all, I was supposed to be in charge now.

'Look here, Yeo,' my colleague replied, 'I may not be much of a geographer, but I can bloody well tell a peninsula from an island.'

I turned to De Freville for support, but he sided with Oakley – I suspected to curry favour.

And there I left the matter. I *was* probably wrong. After all, Oakley had been to sea before, as we had heard: 'in a properly fitted-out and sea-worthy thirty footer'.

At half-past four we glimpsed land ahead for the third time that afternoon. There were dark hills veiled by clouds and a bright shore with palm trees picked out in brilliant sunshine. At one end was a smaller, mist-shrouded island.

According to the chart, Raboa was virtually surrounded by fringing reefs with a break only at its north-eastern corner. I did my best to direct Oakley there and was gratified to find unbroken water stretching away towards a sandy, mangrove shore. Surprisingly, I could see breakers only to starboard. I began to appreciate how difficult it was to judge nautical distances.

Oakley slowed the engine. The old boat forged on gently through shallow, clear water. Doris and De Freville were in the bows, looking out for coral and submerged rocks. I was standing with Oakley in the little deckhouse trying to persuade Oakley to make for a creek that I had spotted through the binoculars. It was while I was doing this that I noticed De Freville gesticulating and, apparently, shouting.

'What did he say?' Oakley shouted.

Several things then happened in quick succession. I put my head round the side of the deckhouse, repeated the question and heard De Freville answer, 'Woah!' Before I could relay this information to Oakley there was a ghastly scraping noise fron beneath the hull, followed by a scream from Doris and a terrible grinding jerk from the stern. The engine raced alarmingly and then juddered to a halt. Simultaneously, Oakley and De Freville snarled at me, 'You bloody idiot.'

In the brief silence which followed I heard for the first

time a shrill whistling call, the like of which I had never known from any bird.

The tide was running in and after about an hour of bitter recrimination the *Bounty II* floated free. Unfortunately, we were unable to start the engine. Something final had evidently happened to it.

We were carried slowly towards the shore. There was no sign of serious damage to the hull and De Freville used the boat-hook to punt us away from some ugly-looking rocks towards a long white beach. *Bounty II* grounded amidst some tall mangroves which we used as a pliant mooring.

The sun was low in the sky when we waded ashore, carrying only enough to enable us to prepare a simple meal.

Ever since Oakley first mentioned the expedition I had imagined, with some misgivings, our arrival on a real desert island. Even so I had never believed that we would be shipwrecked. Not that it was a disaster, of course, but the effect was the same – we were marooned and no one knew where we were.

6

De Freville and I discovered another mutual passion on our first uncomfortable night as castaways.

Doris cooked a hasty supper on the beach. Then, after a swift crimson sunset we all retreated, in gathering dusk, to the security of *Bounty II*. It was only seven o'clock and we were faced with the infinity of a tropical night. We decided to conserve our paraffin and torch batteries and I lay on my narrow bunk in warm darkness, listening to the regular slapping of wavelets against the wooden hull. De Freville was somewhere on deck.

It was then that I heard him humming to himself and, later, break softly into song. The surprising thing was what he was singing; the staggering thing was how he was doing it.

He stopped when he saw my head appear through the hatchway. The scene was now bathed in soft moonlight and I could see him lying on the fo'c'sle, his head propped up on one arm. De Freville regarded me with that look of detached amusement which I had previously found so maddening.

'Was that you singing, De Freville?' His amusement increased at the fatuousness of my question.

'It was, Dr Yeo.'

'But how on earth do you do it? I declare that I would not have believed it possible.'

De Freville ignored my question. The ensuing silence was punctuated by the dripping of water and the creaking of mangrove branches.

I persisted.

'But how, De Freville . . . how?'

He smiled and pulled himself into a sitting position.

'Well, I'm not quite sure, really. When I was sixteen I found some old gramophone records of my father's – seventy-eights they were – and became fascinated and then totally obsessed.' He stopped to lash out at some mosquitoes which had just discovered our presence at the edge of the mangroves.

I waited patiently for him to continue.

'Then I discovered that I could raise the pitch of my voice to something like hers and, after a lot of practice, managed to match her tone. I used to sing along with the recordings until I knew every inflection of the voice.' He paused and examined a bloody mosquito corpse on his finger tip. 'I was very upset when she died . . .'

'Why were you singing "Alabama Song"?' I asked. 'Somehow, I would have thought "Surabaya Johnnie" more appropriate in our situation.'

'You know . . . that thought passed through my mind just as I started "Alabama Song". Fancy you thinking the same.'

It was astonishing how very close we seemed to be in our interests – history, birds and now this. Perhaps that was why we had had our feud. After all, like repels like and all that.

We talked for another half an hour until finally we were driven below by fresh squadrons of voracious mosquitoes. The others were already asleep: Oakley mumbling incoherently and Doris draped half out of a hot sleeping bag.

De Freville and I crawled into our bunks and lay silently in the stuffy darkness. I think I must have dozed. All that I can now remember was an increasing degree of contact with the wooden hull that was the starboard limit of my bunk and the whining of mosquitoes in their relentless quest for blood.

I struggled slowly from a dream of love with a large wooden woman, with close-set eyes, on a flea-ridden mattress – wakened by a sliding noise and a groan from somewhere in the darkness to my left. I might well have resumed my troubled fantasy had it not been for a loud crash, a shout of wild obscenity from Oakley and a stifled scream from Doris.

Strangely, I found it very difficult to turn on my mattress, but somehow managed to push my head over the edge of the bunk. I could make out little in the gloom.

'The fucking boat's on its side,' Oakley bawled into my right ear. He could be a very common little man at times.

I looked at the luminous dial of my watch. It was still only a quarter-past nine.

Bounty II refloated some time before dawn. The relief that this brought was offset by renewed mosquito attacks. It had been a dreadful night. Most of all for Oakley and Doris, who were bundled together on the floor of the tilting cabin.

We waded ashore soon after dawn carrying a primus stove, breakfast food and utensils. A score of Brown Boobies were already feeding out towards the reef. One after another they plunged into the glistening water. I could just detect an occasional high-pitched wheezing call and a faint cackling. It was certainly not the strange whistling which I had heard just after the boat ran aground.

We breakfasted on porridge, coffee and condensed milk, sitting in a row at the top of the beach, shaded by

76

tall palms. To a detached observer it would have seemed idyllic, but not to four disgruntled academics, tired and itching, marooned on a remote Pacific shore with little prospect of immediate rescue.

It was De Freville who took charge on that wretched early morning in paradise. Oakley and Doris were grumbling and arguing about their night on the cabin floor and I was far too dazed to test my frail qualities of leadership.

De Freville outlined a most sensible course of action. He would inspect and, if possible, repair the engine; Oakley was to experiment with the radio and, if he could, make contact with Manau; Doris and I were to establish a camp away from the mosquito-infested mangroves and, if we had time, start off along the shore to look for the two villages shown on the map.

In retrospect, I can see that there were far too many 'ifs' in De Freville's otherwise excellent plan. Doris and I certainly managed to unload most of the equipment and supplies and pitch the tents, but found that we were virtually hemmed in by impenetrable bush and deep channels that made any exploration extremely difficult, if not downright impossible. De Freville discovered that the propeller was sheared off, its shaft snapped and the engine flooded. Oakley managed to extract from the radio some impressive crackling and occasional snatches of conversation from all parts of the world and that was all. The instrument lacked a transmitter.

At supper that evening I again expressed my belief that we were not on Raboa. I argued that two of our sightings of land were not islands, but peninsulas, that we had not seen a village at the eastern end of the island (as we should have if we were on Raboa) and, furthermore, had seen another, smaller, island which was not shown on the map. According to my interpretation of the landmarks, we were on the first of the string of islands, which would explain the remarkably short duration of our voyage.

Oakley would have none of it. We were on Raboa and that was the end of the matter as far as he was concerned. De Freville and Doris seemed too fed-up even to enter the argument. But I was not convinced and I laid out the map again. If my theory was correct we were on Ru-in, and if that was not daunting enough, the small island at the eastern end had no name. It had to be the sacred island on which, according to Rua, the 'old ways' were still practised 'in times of trouble' – and that had included the ritual killing of adulterers.

Our second night as castaways was preceded by an incident which I found especially discomforting. Oakley had brought only two tents and this meant someone was going to have to share one with Doris.

'Well, it's up to you, Doris,' Oakley laughed with quite unnecessary coarseness, 'which of us do you fancy?'

'Really, Oakley . . .' I had begun to protest just as Doris made her choice, without a moment's hesitation.

'Doc,' she announced. 'I'll sleep with you, Doc. Hell, I had enough of Dr Oakley on the cabin floor last night and I don't think Donald's ever really fancied me.'

I was surprised to learn De Freville's first name. *Donald* De Freville. It had a nice ring and, very appropriately, coincided with my changing view of him.

I suspected that Oakley was very put out by Doris's choice, but, if I was right, he skilfully concealed his feelings by jumping to his feet to start bossing us about. He had evidently recovered from his depression of the day before. After all, he maintained that we would soon establish contact with the villagers, who, he still believed, lived at either end of the island.

That evening I tactfully waited for Doris to go into the

tent. The western sky was crimson and gold. I could hear the short nasal call of a heron from the darkness of the mangroves, which seemed strangely sinister in the fading light.

I decided not to sleep in my blue pyjamas that night, merely slipping off my khaki shirt in the warm darkness. The floor was only the area of a double bed and I found it difficult to creep into the tent. I could just make out Doris's form, covered in white sheet and lying on her sleeping bag facing the canvas wall. There was a crinkling noise as my knee squashed down on what I guessed was one of Doris's folded kaftan dresses. Odd that she should bother to wrap it in tissue paper for a jaunt like this. She was not noticeably tidy. Perhaps she had been given it by her sister in Kensington and just stuck it in at the last minute. I zipped up the entrance flaps and lay with my nose pressed to the other wall.

We did not speak, but I was acutely conscious of her presence – her gentle breathing, occasional body movements and, above all, disturbing whiffs of toilet soap. I remember wishing that my shorts were not so infernally long in the legs.

It required no directives from either Oakley or De Freville to convince me of our duties on the following morning. The site which Doris and I had selected was still far too near the mangroves. During the night mosquitoes had poured into our tents. They had even managed to crawl through the zip fastener, as I saw in the torchlight when I vainly attempted to swat the little fiends. And that was not all, there were some very painful skin irritations which seemed to emanate from the sand on which we had pitched the tents. Oakley thought that they were caused by jiggers. Whatever their origin they were hellish and completely dispelled my persisting uneasiness at sharing a tent with a female undergraduate, especially a liberated American one.

Clearly we would have to shift camp. We set about it immediately after a hasty wash and a makeshift breakfast of coffee, oatmeal biscuits and bananas.

It was De Freville who convinced us of the advantages of the hilltop site. This was some half a mile to the east, but close to the beach and near a small mangrove-fringed inlet. The hill was about a hundred feet high, rocky with a light covering of reddish soil and the suggestion of a path through tangled vegetation to a flat summit. Behind was a shallow, boulder-strewn valley which rose steeply on the other side to form the wooded slopes of an immense mist-shrouded mountain.

We loaded our equipment and supplies on to *Bounty II* and, waist-deep in swirling water, dragged and pushed the old craft from her moorings through shallow ebbing water to another mangrove closer to our new camp.

It was well into the afternoon before we humped the last of our gear up the steep rocky slope. We were all hot and tired, but still could not rest for we were faced with another problem – water, or rather the lack of it. The most promising possibility was to explore the inlet near our mooring, and, sure enough, we found that it led to a clear stream which tumbled down from the moist mountain slopes. We filled our plastic containers and hauled them up to the camp. It was an exhausting business and became our most irksome daily chore.

That evening De Freville and I established another routine. It was my idea. I shyly suggested it while we were both washing up in the mangroves just before dusk. I was afraid that he would laugh at my scheme, but he readily fell in with the idea, although we had little chance

80

to discuss it: we were both anxious to avoid the nightly mosquito ordeal.

I decided not to pursue, that night, the matter which De Freville and I had discussed in the damp, spindly gloom of the mangroves. We were all dog-tired, and it would have been difficult for me to broach the subject as we sat together, on our flat hilltop, watching for the third time on the island the last luminous traces of the dying sun.

De Freville and I discussed my project on the following morning as we fetched the water supply for the day. Doris was tidying the camp and Oakley was down in the boat, fiddling with the radio, so we could talk freely as we waded along the inlet and then climbed up to the pool in the mountain stream which was now our watering place.

We agreed that the best situations for what we had in mind would be in the mangroves, during the day, and on the far side of the boulder-strewn valley, in the evening. Both places would be beyond earshot from the camp: the first would be cool in the heat and the other outside mosquito range at night.

There was no opportunity that day for De Freville and me to steal away together, we all had too much to do. Somehow or other we had to break through entangled thorny bush and scale almost vertical mountain slopes, or else find a way along the shore and across high wooded cliffs to find one of Oakley's villages. Not that it would do us a great deal of good if, as I feared, we were not on Raboa, for there were no villages shown on the map for that island. Yet, paradoxically, I was developing the strong, but I admit, quite irrational feeling that we were not alone on the island.

7

It was curious, but for our first days as castaways one or other of us was constantly cross or worried or sulking about something. It was not so much that we got on one another's nerves – although we certainly did that – it was more that we got on our own: in differing degrees, at varying intervals and for all sorts of reasons.

Food was a frequent cause of dissension, especially as our supplies dwindled and we were forced to hunt and gather for ourselves. My aversion to shellfish irritated Oakley, and I could never understand his querulous dislike for porridge (which we possessed in quantity), while De Freville and Doris would argue endlessly about the edibility of the island's invertebrate fauna.

Disputes, however, could flare up on almost any topic. Oakley and De Freville were barely on speaking terms after a difference of opinion about the music of Gilbert and Sullivan which De Freville, predictably, loathed. Oakley and I would regularly niggle away about the precise location of the island, while Doris infuriated Oakley with her views on nuclear disarmament and her belief that the theory of natural selection could not account for the autumnal shrinkage of a species of Polish shrew which she had been told about at Kramer College.

Fortunately, it was unusual for all of us to be out of humour simultaneously. In fact, we tended to take it in turns, so that the sight of Oakley dejected would act as a real stimulus to me while one of Doris's early morning moods could positively enliven De Freville.

It was just such a reaction that caused me to initiate our first real exploration of the island following the relocation of our camp on the hilltop. Oakley had made a desultory and unsuccessful search for some of his weird insects and was much cast down – hence, my spirits rose sufficiently to enable me to get things moving on the afternoon of our third day on the island.

I decided that we should strike out roughly westward along the shore. The tide was ebbing from the mangroves and we squelched along shifting sand with Frigate Birds overhead, accompanied by a score of Sanderling running ahead of us like miniature clockwise toys. Their familiar, insistent calling gave a comfortable feeling of security on that empty tropic beach.

After half an hour or so the mangrove fringe gave way to a fractured rocky shore and then we were faced with the deep, unbroken water of the inlet which Doris and I discovered on our previous excursion. Turning left we scrambled over jagged outcrops and then climbed upwards to the edge of a low, but steep, volcanic cliff. Peering over we looked down on to a narrow strip of mangroves and, a hundred yards or so away, at a long sand shore interspersed with mangroves. To the left there was another cliff, the first inaccessible bastion of the mountain. Behind us was an impenetrable nightmare of thorny bushes and tangled distorted trees.

We could go no further, unable to climb higher or cross to the other side of the channel, which obviously penetrated much further inland. It was an eerie landscape. Only the sunlit shore opposite looked inviting and we could not get to it. I remember thinking that I would never swim across that dark water, even if I could climb down to it.

It was at that precise moment we heard a muffled

echoing sound, almost a deep cough. We heard it only once. It was De Freville who spoke first.

'Well, if I didn't know better I would have said that that sounded like a female crocodile – or Jeremy Bains.' He looked apologetically at Oakley as though some further explanation was necessary. 'I was on the Nile last year with the College expedition. One of the jokes was that Jeremy's cough sounded like a female crocodile.'

'You don't get crocodiles in the sea – stupid.' Doris giggled.

'And there you are wrong, Miss,' Oakley interjected. '*Crocodylus porosus* is a marine species which occurs from the Indian Ocean to, certainly, northern Australia and, I wouldn't be surprised, as far as here. They can swim enormous distances – but I didn't know that they coughed.'

So now there was something else to worry about: not only sea-snakes and sharks (which we had not seen, though I frequently thought about them), but marine crocodiles. I was convinced that they were there. The place was redolent of the beastly things. I imagined pairs of waiting eyes protruding from the water and my legs clamped by huge jaws. It was, of course, an over-reaction, partly, I think, because we were at a cliff edge.

Then the emotional see-saw swung again: my confidence of the early afternoon evaporated while Oakley expatiated, almost exuberantly, on the behaviour, ecology and physiology of large aquatic reptiles. I was surprised that he should talk so volubly about vertebrate animals, for he knew precious little about birds. I supposed that he had mugged it up for one of his Part II lectures.

Perversely, Doris also perked up, claiming that we had found by far the nicest part of the island. In our different ways I think that we were all touched by the atmosphere of the place although none of us could have guessed the role that it was to play in our lives.

That evening De Freville and I slipped off to the far side of the boulder-strewn valley. The depression that we had selected hid us from the camp where Doris and Oakley were sitting before a smoking fire. We were away from the camp for more than three hours and there was no sign of Oakley and Doris when we returned: the fire was smouldering ashes and our companions were asleep in their tents. I paused before retiring and, for the first time on the island, felt in sympathy with the place. The moonlight silhouetted the mangroves against the silvery lagoon. I could just hear the gentle swish of waves. Somewhere to my left came a familiar English sound, the screeching of a Barn Owl.

'What in hell were you two up to last night?' Doris addressed the question as I struggled from sleep into stale overnight air to discover my undergraduate glaring at me, point blank, from her sleeping bag. 'I sat up till after ten. We thought that you were both drowned or lost, or God knows what else.'

I was touched by her concern, but realized the need for a convincing alibi.

'Bird watching,' I mumbled. 'Just bird watching.'

'Bird watching! *In the dark?*'

Fortunately I did not lose my temper at her impertinence and answered in a level voice.

'There was moonlight and we could hear their calls. Quite sufficient for our purposes – I wanted to know what species are out at night.'

'But you didn't even take binoculars,' my indignant

85

tent-fellow persisted. 'And why did you need tissue paper for bird watching? Or listening, if it comes to that.'

'Droppings,' I answered, thinking as quickly as I could. 'Something to wrap up the droppings.'

'Bird droppings? In *my* tissue paper? Yuk.' Doris paused to consider the matter. 'They'd get squashed.'

'Not when they're dry,' I countered. 'Very interesting things, droppings. You can tell what birds have been feeding on – seeds, small bones, all that sort of thing.'

To my relief, Doris's inquisition was interrupted by De Freville bearing mugs of tea.

Doris postponed further questioning until after breakfast.

'I hear that you're into bird droppings, Donald.'

'Well, yes. Very interesting things really, droppings . . .'

'You can tell what they've been eating,' Doris interjected. 'But why in hell wrap them in my tissue paper?'

De Freville shot me a quick glance and retreated to his tent just as Oakley was trying to squeeze out.

Oakley clutched his notebook. He had that sly, satisfied look which he assumed when he was about to announce something important. I could tell this even as he backed out of the tent. His expressive bottom radiated self-importance.

'We shall have to start rationing the food,' Oakley commenced, somewhat put out at being jostled by De Freville during his exit from the tent.

'Clearly we are not going to push our way out of here as easily as I had thought,' Oakley continued theatrically. 'We must hope that some of the villagers will come this way soon. But there can be no certainty and we must husband our resources.'

I was rattled by Oakley's pompous phraseology. Surely things were not that bad.

'We shan't need to do much husbandry if we can live off the island,' Doris retorted briskly.

My heart sank at the prospect. It had occurred to me, even back in College, that sooner or later someone on the expedition would probably start a back-to-nature movement and, although it looked as though we might now have no alternative, I still did not relish the idea. As far as I was concerned food was something that came, neatly packaged, from shops or was served up by candle-light at the High Table. I was squeamish about anything too obviously natural in origins and dreaded the thought of battering fish or strangling Mangrove Herons, let alone shinning up coconut palms.

Doris had no such inhibitions. She was apparently still in her alternative technology phase and welcomed the opportunity to test our skills as hunters and gatherers. We could catch fish, she said, perhaps even try to land a shark or two. There were line and hooks in the fo'c'sle of *Bounty II* and a dangerous-looking catapult that Bogey had thoughtfully, or forgetfully, left on board; we could make spears and set snares; somehow we had to learn to bring down coconuts; there were shellfish and fiddler crabs for the taking.

The prospect of such an uncongenial alteration in our already uncomfortable existence led me to redouble my efforts to persuade my companions to continue exploring the island. I argued that if we devoted ourselves to fishing and coconut-gathering we would have little time to find a way out of the bay in which we were trapped. If Oakley was right, and we were on Raboa, then all would be well; if we were on Ru-in, as I believed, then we might still make contact with someone or other. After all, our map was ten years old and, although there were no villages shown, something might have happened since then.

I further reasoned that exploration could contribute to our original aims – the finding of Oakley's insects and De Freville's Petrel. I was also intrigued by that strange whistling call, which, I was sure, did not come from the beak of any bird that I had ever come across.

Eventually, we compromised. We would do turn and turn about: Oakley and I would explore while De Freville and Doris hunted and fished. On the following day the roles would be reversed. Oakley had jotted down other schemes in his notebook including one to build a large bonfire to generate smoke signals, in case we sighted a passing ship, boat or canoe. We spent the rest of the morning collecting and piling up twigs and branches near the camp.

I was disappointed that De Freville and I were not paired off on the rota. It would have provided marvellous opportunities. However, Doris's idea of a daily siesta gave us the excuse to slip down occasionally to the mangroves. Our alibi was to escape the midday heat on the hilltop plateau and, to carry further conviction, to observe the habits of the Mangrove Heron.

That afternoon Oakley and I waited for the tide to ebb sufficiently for us to walk along the beach to the east. It was a memorable scene. The brilliant white sand was dotted with countless scuttling fiddler crabs and myriad tiny pools reflecting the deep blue of a cloudless sky. The hot salty air was filled with the rasping calls of Sooty Terns flying to and fro from the receding tidal edge. Sanderling were in abundance. I am sure I spotted a Ruddy Turnstone and, just possibly, a Red-necked Stint. We gave a wide berth to a pair of yellow and black sea-snakes wriggling in the outflow from the nearby creek.

The east end of the bay turned out to be almost a mirror image of the one we had explored on the previous day. First, we came to a wide inlet. To our right was a steep rocky shore covered with dense mangroves and backed by a continuum of impenetrable trees and shrubs. There was no way that we could wade across to the facing shore, which differed in detail from that at the west end in being an unclimbable lava cliff. We advanced only a hundred yards or so along the rocky, wooded shore on our side, despite nearly an hour of exhausting clambering, hacking and crawling. It too was a dead-end, another sheer slope climbing up to the shoulder of the mountain.

We were hot and tired when we returned to the camp. There was no sign of the others. At this time on previous days Doris had been busying herself with the primus stove and our supper would have been well under way. It was all very depressing, especially after our wasted efforts of the afternoon.

Doris and De Freville appeared just before dusk. They too were tired and dispirited. It was one of the rare occasions when we were all 'down' together. De Freville was carrying several grey, phallic-shaped invertebrates, one of which heaved in a sinister rhythm, and Doris had a bucketful of gothic-looking molluscs.

8

Oakley vomited at half-past eight, Doris around twenty to nine and De Freville at 8.55. I noted the times exactly because I believed that we should learn as much as we could about the toxic symptoms which I feared we would all be regularly experiencing. I was able to make my observations only because I had been sick after the first mouthful of Doris's nauseating concoction. It was the first time that I had been grateful for what Mother called my 'nervous stomach'.

I was, in fact, nervous about the whole business. What if my companions died? What would the College Council make of the loss of two undergraduates *and* a Fellow? Even when I realized the improbability of this there was the grey prospect of an evening with no possibility of slipping off with De Freville.

Sleep was difficult that night. Doris was in and out for most of the night, Oakley made a fearful fuss just before midnight (it was the first time that I had heard him speak of his *own* rectum) and De Freville was groaning and stumbling about outside during the early hours.

I was relieved when dawn came. It seemed only right that I should prepare breakfast. I carried cups of tea and bowls of porridge to my prostrate companions before the sun had risen far in the sky. Even Oakley was grateful for porridge that morning.

Despite the disastrous effects of her culinary experiment with lower invertebrates, Doris persisted in her intention that we should live 'off' the island. It was a matter of life and death, she said. Our civilized food was dwindling fast. If we didn't experiment then we would never discover what was edible and would very likely perish. It was no good waiting until we were too weak to fend for ourselves.

She went on and on until I could have screamed.

Oakley made it clear that he would not be foraging with me. He was still far too poorly; De Freville clearly had no intention of helping me or of carrying out any exploration that day. I could see that Doris was getting on his nerves as well.

Then Doris let rip. Her rage consumed her like flame on a Christmas tree. She did not shout, in fact she hardly raised her voice at first, but there was no doubt about her feelings, or the nature of her grievance: us.

She started with me.

'Has it ever occurred to you, *Dr* Yeo,' she grated ominously. 'Has it ever remotely dawned on your tidy academic mind just how . . . how *specialized or totally useless you are*.'

Her words hit me like physical blows. De Freville blinked at Doris's bellow, opened his mouth and then closed it, like a sick camel, as she continued at slightly reduced volume.

Doris's delivery to me was in the nature of a prologue: a sort of warm-up before she got round to Oakley and then to poor De Freville's shortcomings. Yet her comtempt cut into me keenly. Her bitter outburst confirmed in a single flash of dreadful insight all that I had slowly come to recognize about myself. It was not only my total failure as a castaway, it was everything else – middle-aged and childless, incompetent, even in that silly business with Muriel Oakley, squatting insignificantly on my academic dunghill. I was useless all right and even if I wasn't, what was there to look forward to? Chairman of the Faculty Board, membership of the Editorial Board of the *Historical Review*? It was just one downhill run to the grave.

I was feeling so sorry for myself that I was unable to grasp the nature of Doris's diatribe on the shortcomings of my fellow castaways and only recall the dramatic climax to her denunciation.

'Screw the Cricklade wool trade, fifteen lousy thirty six to fifteen forty stupid six; screw De Freville's Petrel and Lollardy; most of all, screw insect assholes.'

I must confess that even in the depths of my despair I was shocked by the vulgarity of Doris's tirade and, almost as much, by the poverty of her language. The abuse of the average Tudor serving wench would have been infinitely more inventive and colourful (pimps, lechers, horsecoursers, whoremongers, scallywags . . .). But to poor modern little Doris, standing, arms akimbo, with her dark eyes flashing, like an indignant bantam, it was all 'assholes' and 'screwing'.

Ms Lakowski had not finished with us, not by any means. She now extended her contempt to include the shortcomings of our sex and, finally, our attitudes to her.

'And I know what you really think about me.'

She glared at me.

'Oh yes, you laugh, in your sneaky limey way, at my T-shirts, about feminism and Green Peace and all that – your precious Cecil Fox hinted as much. But at least I *care* about things and I'm not going to sit here and . . . and . . .'

Doris broke off to pick up the plastic bucket and then the axe, which she began to wave above her head to emphasize her points.

'My old man could make mincemeat of you lot – '

'Well, if he's so bloody marvellous why did he send you to study with such a collection of assholes,' De Freville butted in.

'Oh, if you only knew, if you only knew – you might not be squatting so comfortably,' Doris screeched back. 'Now are you going to get off your butts and do something?'

Doris stopped, picked up the fishing line, dropped it in the bucket and advanced on me, still brandishing the axe. I grabbed it from her, more in self-defence than for any other reason, and fled, snatching the bucket as I did so.

So it was that I found myself in the uncongenial role of hunter and gatherer with very bruised feelings and no clear idea where or how to hunt and gather.

I definitely favoured gathering. The trouble was what to gather. Coconuts were totally inaccessible as far as I was concerned and I had already witnessed the consequences of collecting sedentary littoral fauna. So, reluctantly, I became a hunter and headed for the mangroves in a turmoil of mixed emotions.

My approach was marked by a cautious Mangrove Heron and an alert mongoose. Both dissolved into the green, dripping gloom as I drew near. Overhead, an expert, a solitary Swamp Harrier, was quartering in clear morning air. With a heavy heart, I sloshed about in the mangroves for half an hour or more, trying to calm myself. The only visible prey were hundreds of tiny mud skippers (mangrove whitebait?) which flopped swiftly away and sank from view at my clumsy approaches.

All that was left for me was to fish with Bogey's hooks and line.

The most obvious place was a promontory at the east end of the bay which Oakley and I had seen the day

93

before. The sun was directly overhead and it was hot, weary work scrambling over the bare skeleton of that lava outcrop, but I eventually found a convenient niche, shaded by overhanging rock.

I pulverized a large, pale-green winkle, impaled its squirming remains on a rusty hook, cast the line (before succumbing to a brief nausea) and relaxed. For company there was a self-conscious Reef Heron (with the white plumage which Hartlaub recorded as being 'very rare in Manabau') and some inquisitive, blue and red crabs that regarded me suspiciously with long-stalked eyes.

It was a dazzling, almost hypnotic scene. Sunlight glittered on turquoise water and the distant fringe of breakers. A white beach swept away from the fractured black lava to a frieze of grey-green palms, shimmering in midday heat. The only sounds were the lazy swishing of tiny waves and the dry creaking call of passing terns.

I was lulled by feelings of unreality, dozing and dreaming in my rocky nook, for how long I am not sure, but, gradually, reality returned bringing those uneasy feelings of apprehension and fraudulence which have always dogged me. What on earth was I doing in this place? How could I possibly be expected to deal with a struggling and, for all I knew, a large and dangerous fish?

At that very moment the line jerked alarmingly. Fortunately, and prudently, I had wound it several times around a rocky spur and jammed the wooden stick, to which it was tied, into a convenient cleft. I had no intention of touching that wildly gyrating line, a decision which was reinforced by occasional glimpses of a dark, triangular fin. Clearly, the only rational course of action was to wait until the fish exhausted itself, escaped, or, perhaps, had a heart attack.

None of these things happened. Instead, an even larger

black triangle appeared, travelling at tremendous velocity towards my jerking line. Fortunately, I picked up the hatchet with the intention of cutting free the line. But events moved too swiftly for me. A demented, greyish shark landed lashing at my feet in a desperate attempt to escape from an even larger monster whose head momentarily broke the surface. I hit out wildly with the hatchet before collapsing.

It took me several minutes to recover, lying shaken and soaking with sweat on the harsh lava.

Slowly I realized that all was as it had been before. Terns were overhead, the turquoise lagoon still glittered in the hot sun. Only the Reef Heron had departed, and at my feet lay the lifeless body of a small shark, barely four feet long, its head disfigured by a single ugly gash.

I humped the unfortunate fish across the reef and along the shore, before pausing to rest in some mangroves. I was exploding hot and bathed my face in muddy water. It was shortly after this that I noticed a remarkable thing. About two hundred yards away was a row of palm trees which had been pushed sideways by hurricane or earthquake and were now growing with their leafy crowns close to the steep hillside. They were loaded with coconuts. Afterwards, I heard, for the third time, the strange whistling call.

The bringing home of the shark was a moment of great pride and the reactions of the castaways were gratifying in the extreme. They were lying in the tents when I called to them. Doris was the first to emerge: she seemed to have recovered from her early-morning rage.

'Doc, you clever old guy,' she called. 'Donald, come and see what he's got, *and* you, Dr Oakley.'

From her tone, I guessed that my colleague had entertained sarcastic doubts on my hunting abilities. Oakley could be very petty if things were not going his way.

De Freville put the kettle on the primus while Doris got to work on the shark. I had become quite attached to my burden and was forced to turn away from its butchery. After tea, I announced, with such nonchalance as I could muster, that I would be off to see what else could be found.

An hour later I reappeared bearing four large coconuts in a sack. Even Oakley was impressed and De Freville's reaction clearly indicated that our differences concerning Bastard Feudalism were now entirely forgotten.

That evening Doris cooked shark steaks in coconut milk. We gnawed away at the coconut flesh for dessert. After supper De Freville and I slipped off for a couple of hours. I even managed to extract another piece of tissue paper from Doris, who made only a few derogatory comments about 'goddam bird droppings'.

Despite my success as a hunter and a gatherer, Doris still pursued a remorseless quest for fresh island foods – although even this led to more worries. I must confess that I was rattled next morning when I found her cooking mud in the frying pan. She had taken the stuff from the mangroves and had formed it into pats. At first I thought that she was cleaning rust from the pan and only realized her purpose when she carefully laid the hot grey discs in a mess tin. They stank revoltingly. Yet, after they had cooled, Doris started to nibble one. She had, apparently, read in the *New York Times* that in one of the southern states (Mississippi, she thought) some of the poor whites regularly ate mud. They dug it from special places. It was supposed to contain some essential nutrients and, according to Ms Lakowski, these would soon be in very short supply.

Doris also spent hours practising with the catapult and became astonishingly proficient. Her first victim was a

Red-throated Lorikeet, which she knocked down at a range of twenty-five feet. Shortly after, she slew two Wattled Honeyeaters and, some days later, stunned and wrung the neck of a Polynesian Triller. De Freville and I measured the corpses and collected ectoparasites, but it was distressing work for ornithologists and the half-cooked flesh made little impression on our appetites.

Fortunately we were improving as fishermen. We frequently caught parrot fish from the reefs while Oakley became a resourceful shellfisherman. Doris concocted passable chowder from large clams that Oakley levered from rock pools at the east end of the bay, all the while grumbling about her sexist role as cook. Fruit and vegetables were problems, for there was nothing we could be sure was edible, apart from the coconut flesh which Doris contrived to introduce into most of our meals. An exception was a sort of scraggy parsnip which De Freville discovered growing among tall grasses in damp soil on the way to our watering place. It had heavy, close-textured flesh – rather like the cassava that Rua had cooked for us. Doris sliced it thinly and boiled it in diluted sea water, but it made exhausting, tasteless eating and I dreaded its regular appearance in our diet.

For me, those appalling island foods were the most trying thing about our situation. I watched, with apprehension and increasing depression, the dwindling of our stores. We kept an emergency stock of canned meats and packet soups, and the porridge oats and tea bags lasted well, but inexorably our food deteriorated to a range of unappetizing marine invertebrates, coconuts and De Freville's parsnips, a bizarre assortment of fish and occasional unlucky birds slaughtered by Doris. The only local food that I enjoyed was Doris's clam chowder, and even that palled.

I would have given anything for an average-to-poor College lunch. Oakley took to reminiscing about notable College Feasts of the past decade. De Freville confessed to an insatiable desire for egg and chips.

Doris regarded such fantasies as a reflection on her cooking. Sometimes she seemed almost to enjoy our predicament. Doris had originally intended spending the vacation at Trenton, Nebraska, with a group dedicated to alternative technology. This would no doubt have involved her in equally appalling culinary experiences.

It was her mud-nibbling that worried me, as it did De Freville, who revealed his misgivings to me one hot afternoon in the mangroves. He had not discussed the matter with Oakley, he told me, but he was becoming increasingly convinced that Doris was pregnant.

De Freville made a convincing case. What disturbed him most were those kaftan dresses. Doris had never worn anything else since she had been on the expedition, whereas in College she invariably appeared in tight-fitting jeans. Not that this meant much, by itself. I think it was just another one of her phases. Yet it *was* odd that she should want to look like a bell tent and, on one occasion (when De Freville had accidentally come across her swimming near the mangroves) she had seemed quite thick around the middle. Furthermore, De Freville, like me, had noticed how poorly Doris seemed in the mornings and there was this ridiculous mud-nibbling. His sister had developed exactly the same bizarre feeding habits during her pregnancy: she had eaten soil when she and her husband had spent a weekend with the De Frevilles in Gloucestershire.

'And there's another thing,' De Freville continued, kicking at a wet mangrove root in obvious embarrass-ment. 'I promised Doris that I wouldn't mention it, but it *is* relevant and I think that you should know about it.'

De Freville looked away and continued his onslaught on the mangrove root.

'Well?' I demanded in some apprehension.

'Footprints,' De Freville whispered.

'Footprints?'

'Yes, footprints. Doris told me that she had seen some footprints in wet sand on the other side of Crocodile Creek. She says she saw them quite clearly through the binoculars. The funny thing is that she seemed quite upset and made me promise not to alarm you and Dr Oakley by telling you about them.'

'But why should we be alarmed and, if it comes to that, why should she?'

'Well, that's the whole point – that's what I'm worrying about – because I went off like a shot and I couldn't see any footprints. Mind you, the tide had turned by the time I got there and they could have been covered up. But why all the mystery? And when I got back she said that she must have been mistaken and that I was to keep quiet about the whole business.'

Finally, De Freville argued remorselessly, there was the extremely odd manner in which Doris had joined the expedition. Like me, De Freville had had only the vaguest idea of the arrangements for the expedition. He had not know until a week before that I was going to Manabau and had only been told that Doris was coming the day before we left.

De Freville said that Oakley had been quite unnecessarily embarrassed about Doris's inclusion and, oddly, had stressed that I should not be told about it – even at that eleventh hour. De Freville suspected that the whole thing had been some sort of last-minute panic to cover up God knows what scandal.

De Freville obviously did not know of Cecil Fox's

malign influence. Yet Doris's appearance had certainly been mysterious. I recalled Oakley's evasive explanation when I had tackled him on the matter high over the Atlantic. With a shock, like a blow, I also remembered something else: the night of the Fellows' Christmas Dinner when Oakley had slept in College and the following morning those muffled excuses and mysterious moving of furniture when I had knocked at his door. I had seen Doris on Oakley's staircase the previous night.

Good God, it didn't bear thinking about. It would have been seven months before. Surely she would be bigger by now if something had happened that night? Yet her attitude to Oakley was pretty off-hand: she had not wanted to share the tent with him and, I suspected, there had been some sort of unpleasantness between them when I had been away catching the shark. But this might just mean that they had fallen out after the event, so to speak.

I did not reveal my fears to De Freville. After all he was only an undergraduate and, really, I found it hard to believe that someone so vivacious and young as Doris could have been involved with my bumptious middle-aged colleague.

Whatever the sordid details, De Freville's general reasoning was convincing because it explained so much that was otherwise inexplicable, especially apparent hallucinations about footprints in the sand. However, I did not want him to know this – not at that stage, at least – so I muttered about 'circumstantial evidence' and squelched off into the searing midday heat.

It was all so damned worrying. As if we were not in sufficient trouble and now there was the possibility, or perhaps even the likelihood, of childbirth under quite impossible circumstances. We had no necessary equipment and could hardly feed a baby on coconut milk. I couldn't even discuss it with Oakley – it would have been too hideously embarrassing. I suppose that I just did not want to admit the awful prospect which De Freville's logic had revealed to me.

9

Doris's condition was not my only medical preoccupation. Despite the liberal application of ointments, my shoulders, arms and thighs had reddened, blistered and then peeled horribly; my ankles, lacerated by jagged lava, nourished a cloud of ravenous flies; Oakley's left buttock had been invaded by a jigger; Doris's ankles had mysteriously swollen; De Freville was troubled by the aftermath of the sandfly onslaught on his abdomen during our second night on the island.

We were a sorry lot. De Freville and Oakley had given up shaving and Doris was distinctly scruffy. I was lethargic and constipated. To make matters worse the mangrove mosquitoes had discovered the camp and our itching faces were again mottled with bumps and scratches. At night we sat in the protective lee of a smoking fire and permeated the tents with acrid smoke before retiring, half-asphyxiated, at the unearthly hour of eight o'clock. The daily chores involved longer and longer treks in blazing heat to collect firewood, to fish from the reefs, fetch the water, dig up De Freville's obnoxious parsnips and search for coconuts.

Oakley had abandoned all pretence of scientific research. We were now only concerned with survival and the prospect of rescue. De Freville organized a regular watch from the camp and each day one or other of us would walk along the shore and up to Crocodile Creek.

My only diversion at that time was the occasional session in the mangroves with De Freville and even these were increasingly subject to sarcastic remarks from Doris. On two occasions she made quite unnecessarily embarrassing scenes when she discovered that I had purloined more of her dwindling supply of tissue paper.

The hot, weary days passed, and life became more and more tiresome. Like the castaways on Shakespeare's enchanted isle we were confused, worried and, I began to feel, increasingly divided amongst ourselves. Worst of all, my digestive processes were in permanent disarray. It had never occurred to me feel much sympathy for those poor sixteenth-century mariners, tormented by Prospero's silly magic, but at least they were not troubled with their bowels and Miranda was not obviously in the family way.

It was late afternoon, three days after my row with Doris about the tissue paper. Faint stains of apricot and gold were colouring the sky in the west. For the first time since we had been on the island, the mists had completely cleared from the mountain slopes and left them dark green and mysterious-looking. The square summit was a mosaic of mellow light and deep blue shadows. A warm, salt breeze ruffled the nearby palms and lazily twirled the smoke from the fire.

Oakley was sitting at the entrance to his tent trying unsuccessfully to ease an embedded thorn from his left instep with his Swiss Army knife. I had noticed that he had been hobbling since the previous morning. He grunted occasionally with pain, but managed to argue with De Freville about the edibility of jellyfish.

Then I spotted Doris, a miniature tent-like figure about two hundred yards away, hurrying back to the camp from the eastern beach. I abandoned my day-dream of a comfortable armchair and a large brandy and rose wearily from the makeshift seat that we had made from duck boards wrenched from *Bounty II*.

Doris waved and then was hidden from view by a clump of tree ferns. I waited, full of foreboding. In less than three minutes she had breasted our hill and immediately began waving again.

'There's a turtle close to the shore,' she bawled, 'about a mile down the beach. It's a monster.'

No one replied. Then Oakley put down his knife and shouted, 'What sort?'

'*I* don't know what sort. It's enormous. And it's goofing about only a few yards out.'

Oakley growled and stirred petulantly. 'I can't get down there until I've finished my foot. You'd all better go. Take the rope with you.'

Doris snatched the carving knife, scooped up a mouthful of water from the bucket and was off down the rocky slope – with remarkable agility for someone in her condition, I thought. De Freville followed with the rope slung over his shoulder. I stumbled along at the rear, showering him with stones and red earth whenever I lost my footing on the slope.

We sighted the creature as soon as we cleared the eastern edge of the mangroves. It was further down the beach, some seventy yards out, a low, grey shape in the water. It looked strikingly like a slug on a piece of mottled glass. As we got nearer, its shape changed and appeared more like a seal, low in the water with its arched body awash. Then, closer still, I could see that its dark glistening back was speckled with white and raised into several smooth ridges extending from its head to its tail. Through the binoculars I was able to catch a glimpse of a blunt head with small piggy eyes and a pinkish throat. It turned its head from side to side in a preoccupied way.

'Christ, it's a leatherback,' De Freville said. 'It must be seven or eight feet long.'

'What in hell is it fooling around like that for?' Doris asked. 'Shall we go in and give it the works?'

'No. It's going to come ashore. My grandad saw them once. It's in his diary – occasionally they nest on the islands . . .'

For an hour or more we stood on the shore as the tide ebbed and the light began to fail. The air was filled with the rasping calls of Sooty Terns. No one spoke much. We were all mesmerized by the great beast rolling in the surf. De Freville whispered that the natives called them Mara and believed that they were possessed of the souls of the long dead.

'The hell with that,' Doris said. 'I'm going back to grab some lights. This could go on all night and I *need* some turtle soup.' She vanished into the dusk.

At once, as though sensing the departure of a hostile force, the great creature began to swim slowly and deliberately towards the beach. After a few seconds it grounded and remained motionless in the wash. The tide seemed to be on the point of turning. The monster was visible only as a dark mound at the water's edge. Then after a few minutes it made a great heaving movement and pushed into the wet sand with all four limbs together.

It came out of the water like an amphibious tank, glistening in the twilight. Its huge flippers were pounding the sand and I realized that the brute was lurching intently towards me. I fell over backwards, and found myself looking straight into its wizened face. The creature stopped for a second, panting and choking with effort, as I edged carefully away over the wet sand squeezing the water from my trousers. Then it turned and crashed its

way up the incline in a slow zig-zag, grunting and threshing at the sand. It ignored us. I crept carefully to within a
yard of it. Its back was nearly waist high. The beach was
flatter here and sloped gently up towards a line of distant
palm trees which were invisible now in the darkness. The
monster paused for a full minute when it reached the line
of high-tide wrack before pushing forward, threshing its
flippers in the powdery sand.

It was then that we heard Doris shouting somewhere to
our right and saw the intermittent flashing of a torch
beam. Further away was the dim yellow glow of a
hurricane light. We called softly back and continued our
watch, too absorbed to pay her much attention: the
beast began to sweep the sand backwards with powerful
movements of its front flippers like huge shovels.

By the time Doris arrived with Oakley the animal was
moving its hind flippers and tail from side to side.

'Good God, it's a whopper.' Oakley held the lamp
above his head and spoke in a low voice. 'Shall we get it
over with? It's getting late.'

'What do you mean *it*?' I was annoyed at the interruption and did not realize what he meant.

'Not now,' De Freville said in a fierce whisper. 'Let her
lay her eggs first.'

Then I realized what Oakley intended to do. Like me,
he was obviously excited by the vast creature and its
aloof preoccupation – but in a very different way. I had
been so taken out of myself by the silence and the
darkness and the mysterious blind movements of the
turtle that I was shocked by Oakley's talk of killing.

He held the lamp head-high above the great reptile,
which had ceased moving its flippers and was now pushing
its tail carefully into the sand. The soft guttering light
picked out the white speckling on its back, which

106

resembled tough rubber. The beast closed its eyes as its tail probed the yielding sand. The lids formed curious narrow vertical slits and the eyeballs seemed to sink into its head. Then the probing stopped, and the flippers recommenced their regular sweeping motion, flinging the sand grains against my feet and legs and stinging like hail. I stepped backwards on to Oakley's bad foot. He swore and pushed me away so that I almost fell on to the labouring animal.

The creature kept grunting like a muffled pig. The waves hissed and broke away down the beach and Oakley complained from time to time about the lateness of the hour, the ache in his foot and the fatigue of holding the hurricane lamp. There was no other noise.

At about half-past ten, the turtle, by now crusted all over with sand, began to push with its massive paddle-like hind flippers, one after the other, stopping occasionally to thrust downwards with its tail. Then the digging started. Each hind flipper curled round alternately to lift the sand from a cavity that deepened steadily. The unoccupied flipper was used each time to sweep the excavated sand aside. The turtle's eyes narrowed during each of these kicking movements, making it look curiously like the University Reader in Agricultural Ergonomics. Simms had a subtle reptilian quality about the face and invariably squinted when making a serious point to the Governing Body.

Then to my surprise the creature began to cry. Great tears flowed down its wrinkled cheeks and hung in long sandy strings as the turtle, still grunting, painfully enlarged the cavity into a heart shape. Gradually the digging slowed. The rear of the sand-covered body sagged into the hole, and finally came to rest. The turtle spread

107

its hind flippers out behind it and slowly lowered its tail into the hole, which was now the depth of a man's arm.

We stood – four voyeurs – at the edge of the small circle of light. I have always been squeamish about the means of procreation: even the thought that my breakfast egg had been extruded, dung-daubed, from a warm female tube could upset me on queasy mornings. Yet I stood absorbed on the empty shore as the great creature prepared for the climax of her labours.

The first eggs appeared within a couple of minutes. There were two of them, white and glistening – like yielding billiard balls. They dropped a foot or more on to the damp sand. But the cascade that followed was astonishing – one, two or three eggs at a time, at ten- or twenty-second intervals showered into the pit. At each deposition the great body lifted slightly. Occasionally, for no obvious reason, the turtle raised its head abruptly and gazed unseeingly into the lamplight, long sandy strips swinging from its eyes. Poor beast, I had a strong desire to touch her ugly reptile head.

Oakley leaned over and said in a whisper that the tears were to do with salt secretion. I wished that he would go away.

There were more than a hundred glistening orbs lying in the damp pit when the turtle started to fill it in, the hind flippers working alternately to pull in the loose piled sand. Every now and again she would beat down with the flippers. They made exactly the same satisfying thump as a child's spade when it whacks the wall of a sandcastle firm and solid. I remembered my mother in a deckchair at Tenby watching me on another beach so many years before.

More stinging sand was suddenly flung against my legs as the leatherback moved her great front limbs. In the lamplight I could see the beach for yards around covered with scattered sand. Gradually she began to move, slowly pushing forward with powerful swimming movements of her front flippers, the long tears still hanging from her eyes.

I had never been held so breathless as by that vast weeping reptile beside the empty sea. The smooth soft skin beneath her immense barrel-shaped body was raw and bleeding from her efforts. Mara, De Freville had said they were called in the islands – the spirits of the dead. There were raised voices and movement near at hand but I was only dimly aware of them.

It was Oakley's shouting in my ear that brought me abruptly to my senses.

'OK,' he was saying, 'let's get it on its back.' He was actually pushing at its huge side. I did not want to understand.

'We'll never do it,' De Freville shouted, 'she's too damned heavy.'

He was pushing too. Doris hovered, long-skirted and witch-like, her dark hair flying, at the edge of the swaying circle of light which glittered softly on the long knife in her hand.

I knelt down at the great beast's side with some feeble intention of protecting her. The skin of her belly was velvety beneath my hand. I was shaking.

Then Oakley jumped astride the creature, her head was between his short fat legs. He pulled her head back, and I could see her skinny neck straining pathetically like a hosepipe. I grabbed Oakley by the leg and pulled. His hair was orange in the lamplight and stood straight up from his head. I seemed to be shouting a good deal and he was shrieking, 'Let go, you bloody fool', while Doris put the knife into his hand.

She covered her face and mumbled something.

I seized Oakley's wrist – I thought I might sink my teeth into it – but De Freville pulled me violently away. Oakley plunged the blade down and then drew it back in a long slow movement, like the bowing of a cellist. A dark red stream shot upward into the lamplight. Oakley put his head down and caught the bloody jet in his open mouth like a child at a drinking fountain.

'It's warm – and quite sweet,' he shouted.

The great body was still moving slowly towards the dark sea, the flippers pushing jerkily against the scattered sand. I turned into the darkness and vomited.

10

Later that night I found myself on the edge of the mangroves. The tide was running in and the darkness was alive with gentle ploppings. Waxy leaves made a soft rustling as the water level rose; small waves slapped against spindly roots. My hands were still shaking. The night had been hot, but I felt chilled; there was a pain in my chest and the back of my head was numb. I knelt on a patch of wet sand and crouched at the water's edge. The flooding tide drove me back. I must have waited there for an hour or more before I felt calm enough to face the others. I spotted the hilltop light as soon as I cleared the mangroves. To my dark-adapted eyes its feeble glow was as dazzling as a lighthouse as I groped and stumbled through spiky scrubs and tangled grass and then up the familiar rocky path.

There was no one about. Oakley's blood-stained sweat shirt and shorts lay on the ground. The light cast jagged shadows on the red stony soil.

I sat on our makeshift seat to remove my sandals and sponge blood from my lacerated legs with the tea towel.

'Doc?'

Doris's voice was low, almost a whisper.

'Doc, are you OK?'

'Yes. Everything's under control . . . more or less.'

'I've been trying to keep awake for you. Where in hell have you *been*, anyway?'

'I just wanted to be quiet for a while.'

'Well, just hit the sack, for God's sake.'

A Barn Owl screeched in the darkness on the other side of the hill. I turned out the lamp and trod in the frying pan. No one woke, and after a time I went into the tent.

'You'll have to get a grip on yourself, Doc, if you're going to stand this racket,' Doris said as I struggled into my sleeping bag.

'*You* didn't fancy being chief executioner.'

'Yeah, well . . .'

I could hear the owl hunting just above the tent.

'Here, give me a paw,' Doris whispered.

Her groping hand drew mine into her sleeping bag. I felt the softness of her breast and the stiffness of a nipple beneath my palm.

'Now go to sleep. Think of the Peasants' Revolt.'

Almost at once her breathing changed, and became soft and regular – she was out like a light. But sleep did not come to me. My right arm was at an extremely awkward angle inside my undergraduate's sleeping bag.

What would Cecil Fox have made of this predicament or my cowardly retreat to the mangroves – assuming that we got back to England and that he ever heard about it? ('I understand, Yeo, that you sought, as it were, sanctuary in the mangroves after your quest for turtle soup.' Christ!) Perhaps he had had me invited to join the expedition merely to give me an unparalleled opportunity to make a spectacular ass of myself, with his favourite tutorial pupil on hand as irritant and spy. Yet he could not have expected that De Freville and I would be so swiftly reconciled. Neither could I have predicted that De Freville would assist in bloody murder. The turtle's belly had been softer than Doris's breast beneath my hand and its eyes had sunk into its head when it laid the eggs.

I had not turned a hair when Doris murdered the

112

Wattled Honeyeaters or the Polynesian Triller. Yet I had panicked completely on the beach that night and afterwards sat weeping in the mangroves. Now here I was experimenting stealthily with Doris's nipple. Could it tell me if she was pregnant? It seemed quite large. And what was all that business about the footprints on the other side of Crocodile Creek? Why did she not want De Freville to tell me and Oakley about them?

My arm had gone numb. I pulled it back into my sleeping bag and dreamed of Oakley and Cecil Fox, in scarlet gowns and khaki shorts drinking goblets of turtle blood at the Fellows' Christmas Dinner.

De Freville had said that it was bad luck to kill a Mara and as things turned out he was right.

I was the first up next morning. It was warm and the sun was already high in the sky. I put on the kettle for a breakfast of weak tea and watery porridge. Doris was next up. She looked tired, but gave me a wink and picked up Oakley's binoculars.

'It's still there,' she said, pointing to the east, 'just above the high-tide line.'

I knew what she was talking about, but had no intention of looking. I had just noticed something very odd: there was no bird song – not a trill, a chirrup or a squeak – only the low murmur of distant surf with not a Swamp Harrier or a Bulbul in sight. The last sign of life had been the screeching of the owl in the night. The island was mute and, for me, dominated by a dark shape on the empty shore.

Then Doris's hectoring shattered the morning stillness.

'Come on, you guys . . . *Come on* . . . She'll be *stinking* before you carve her up.'

113

There was a convulsive movement inside the unopened tent.

'Will you *move* your *ass*, Donald?' Doris bawled at the canvas gable end.

De Freville appeared abruptly: he looked dreadful, his long face grimed and still dazed with sleep.

'*And* you, Dr Yeo . . .' Doris dropped her voice and muttered, 'And Count Dracula', between her teeth.

I suppose I should have remonstrated with Doris, but our relationship had evidently changed and I did not feel well-disposed towards Oakley that morning.

The others seemed unaware of the strange silence. This was hardly surprising, for Doris was making a tremendous noise. She was clearly excited at the prospect of so much animal protein. A thousand pounds of reptile flesh to be dissected, carved, laid out in the sun and cut up for steaks and no doubt for homemade footwear. Here was self-sufficiency in a big way and Doris was going to make the most of it: the Mara had not died in vain as far as she was concerned.

She took charge that morning. We hardly had time to gulp down what passed for breakfast. Oakley was ordered to the corpse, armed with the axe and the carving knife, while she and De Freville were to fetch the day's water supply before joining Oakley in his butcher's yard. I was tactfully left to tidy up the camp site, and then root around for De Freville's awful vegetable in preparation for a evening blow-out of turtle flesh and parsnips.

Oakley left first, not for butchery, but heading for the mangroves to wash his blood-stained garments: he just *had* to get them clean, he said, then he would get to work on the leatherback. He waddled away in the clear early sunlight, gingery and still pompous but somehow oddly subdued with an almost apologetic look as he turned away. Doris and De Freville went off together, laughing, she with a green plastic water-container lifted on to her head like an Indian woman. I watched it bob up and down and then slowly disappear below the edge of the hill as she descended the rocky path.

The silence returned; even the insect hum was subdued. A pencil of smoke from the fire rose straight in the hot still air and mists hung in ragged spirals on grey-green mountain slopes. A haze obscured the barrier reef; the surf was barely audible.

I collected the scattered cups and plates and piled them in the washing bowl with a clatter that made me jump. There was no sign of the squabbling mynahs which usually rent the air with their squawks. As an ornithologist, I suppose that I should have realized the significance of those garrulous scavengers, which had adopted us a week or so before, but certainly not on that silent morning, when they too had made themselves scarce.

I had recovered from my shock of the night before. What a fool I had been. Thank God I was not going to be up to my armpits in turtle blood. How on earth were they going to carry back all that flesh before it rotted in the heat? Her eggs were still in the sand. I would see to it that her youngsters made it back to the sea – if we were still alive by then. I wondered how long they would take to hatch? I would bet that leatherbacks were a protected species. It wouldn't look very good for Oakley if it ever got out that he had killed one. I could use that to shut him up in case he was ever tempted to gossip to Cecil Fox about my part in the proceedings.

Comforted, I turned to lift the bucket. I could see Oakley crouching at the edge of the mangroves. Why was he so agitated about those blood stains? He seemed more like Lady Macbeth than a marooned academic.

11

Oakley had just started to wash his blood-stained T-shirt in the mangroves when the tidal wave struck the island. The force of the water carried him upwards and backwards, stranding him high on the slender sagging branches like a crab on a laurel bush. He clung on desperately for a few seconds, then slid awkwardly down some twenty feet, his stubby arms and legs threshing, and disappeared into a whirlpool of foaming amber water and broken mangrove roots.

I had just finished washing up the breakfast things, pleasantly aware of the lagoon sparkling in the sultry heat. The next moment the rising tide had receded clean out of sight as if by a piece of trick photography. For an instant I glimpsed the muddy seabed. Oakley stood tranfixed on the mire, surrounded by slapping, stranded fish. It was really too shocking to take in during so brief a space of time. Then the landscape before me was blotted out by a surge of water, so gigantic that I was sure it would swallow up the whole island.

The wave had appeared at the edge of the lagoon, raced forward – it must have been travelling at more than a hundred miles an hour – and smashed into the island. The palm trees at the top of the beach were pushed flat by the advancing wall of water. Tree ferns and shrubs were uprooted and flung forward in the boiling torrent. The noise was like the roar of a dozen approaching jet engines.

I was standing at what I sensed was going to be the

final point of impact and yet unable to move a muscle, even to fling myself to the ground. In my initial fright I had kicked over the washing-up bowl and trodden on Oakley's Leitz binoculars. I can still recall their uncomfortable, lumpy feel in the wet soil beneath my sandalled right foot as the watery avalanche crashed against the hill, surged around it and then, miraculously, subsided.

It took me some seconds to realize that I was not, after all, to be swept away. Then I slumped to the ground, picked up Oakley's muddy binoculars and began to search the sodden landscape.

I was convinced that I had seen the last of Oakley for there was no sign of him in the shattered aftermath of the deluge and there was no time to search, for the sea was again pulling back from the lagoon. This was no retreat but a gathering of power. Within minutes the mass of water was flung back at the broken shore. Once more it ebbed before surging in, with diminished force, for what proved to be the last onslaught.

I waited anxiously as the drowned landscape slowly drained. The only sound was the trickling of innumerable murky rivulets. A solitary Swamp Harrier appeared hovering in the still hot air against a backdrop of mist-shrouded mountain slopes. Before me was a muddy devastation of broken mangrove branches, scattered boulders and scarred red earth. The air was heavy with the smell of decaying vegetation swept from the mangrove mud. Dozens of tiny lizards skipped and slithered just below me; a green tree skink stepped delicately across the shattered remains of an uprooted tree fern; the sodden corpse of a Mangrove Heron floated in a muddy pool.

The astonishing thing was that the waves seemed to

have been aimed directly at us, for to the west, and further away at the other end of the bay, the palms were erect and dark-green mangroves still fringed the sea's edge. I suppose that this must have been caused by the shape of the reefs and the shallowness of the lagoon which directed and amplified the ocean shock waves.

It was while I was pondering these matters that I spotted Oakley's body draped over a nasty-looking thorn bush immediately below me. I lost no time in scrambling down to him and, with great difficulty and some minor lacerations, managed to extract him. I pulled aside shattered branches and laid him on a wet expanse of gravelly red soil. I had no idea how to give artificial respiration, but put my hands on his wet chest and pumped it up and down.

My colleague stirred and pushed me away before flopping back, his eyes still closed. His pudgy hands were shaking, a fringe of gingery hair was sticking to his forehead and his normally spruce moustache was covered with a muddy foam. After a few minutes he sat up on his haunches and began quietly swearing to himself in the humid heat.

It took some time to get the sodden, mud-stained Oakley on to his feet and to start up the steep rocky path to our camp. He was tottering, with seaweed stuck behind his left ear, but still very spry for someone I had thought most certainly drowned.

'Take it steady, old chap,' I counselled as he slumped down into a sitting position.

Some of my loathing for Oakley dissolved. I remembered with shame how I had blazed up at him on the beach the night before.

I got Oakley on to his feet again and continued our slow ascent. It was a most difficult business. The steep track was only wide enough for one person. My right side was lacerated by innumerable thorns, bayonet-like twigs and tangled creepers; Oakley was in danger of slipping down a hundred feet or more in a cascade of tumbling stones.

'Christ almighty!'

Oakley's exclamation nearly made me shove him down the stony precipice. I was hot and very fatigued. It was as much as I could do to lower him once more on to the path and look in the direction in which he was excitedly gesticulating.

'The bloody boat's gone.'

Oakley was quivering with agitation. His face was beaded with sweat and I noticed that he now had a large dark patch on the seat of his baggy khaki shorts.

I peered down at the devastated shore. Oakley's observation was not strictly accurate. The boat was still there, but in scattered white fragments tangled up with boulders and uprooted mangroves.

'*Now* what the hell are we going to do?' Oakley shrieked.

The sight of my colleague in such panic produced in me a perverse and quite uncharacteristic calm. Oakley told me the next morning that even in his half-drowned condition it was, for him, one of the most surprising aspects of the whole affair, especially after the appalling scene of the day before. I can't recall exactly what I said, but I remember pointing out that our situation was, in reality, little changed: the boat's engine had seized up (finally as far as we were concerned) and we had unloaded our stores and carried them up to the camp. The most serious loss was the radio, but we hadn't been able to establish contact with anyone, even when it was intact. Our only communications with the outside world had been to listen to a biochemist from Boston who had regaled a fellow radio-ham in Dubai (and whoever else was tuned in) with some very funny Jewish jokes and to an Ecuadorian philatelist from Quito.

It seemed to me, as I emphasized to Oakley, that we should be more concerned about the effects of the tidal wave on the main island. If there was widespread devastation there, then we might well be forgotten. I was not convinced that they would have bothered about us unduly, even without a tidal wave. Furthermore, despite Oakley's earlier confidence, I was still convinced that we were not on the right island. So in the unlikely event of a search party being sent out we would not be found.

My reasoning had a most depressing effect on Oakley. However, I quite understood, for we had all been under considerable strain. My tottering, sodden companion was unrecognizable as the bouncy academic who had broached the idea of the expedition as we sat in the candlelight, drinking claret after the Fellows' Christmas Dinner. He grumbled and cursed as he stumbled along behind me.

I was also very worried about the others. They would have been protected from the full force of the tidal wave at the waterfall, but it was difficult to predict what might have happened when such a huge weight of water struck the island.

Doris was, however, waiting for us, knife in hand, left arm akimbo, when we shambled back into the camp. De Freville was slumped on the ground, head in hands.

'Did either of you assholes think to pick up any stranded fish on your way back? It looks like we've lost our dinner.'

Doris's behaviour was really becoming insupportable. I doubt whether in the history of the College two Fellows had been so addressed by an undergraduate as we had recently. I began to wonder whether the admission of women, for which I had been a vociferous advocate, had been such a good thing. She had changed so much since we had been on the island.

She busily decapitated, gutted and split half a dozen still twitching fish which she had picked up on her way back. After I had seen Oakley safely into his tent, I watched her as, pink and perspiring, she laid out strips of flesh in two neat rows, to dry in the hot sun. When she had finished, we made a pot of weak tea, gnawed away at coconut flesh and then walked down the steep path to the shore and picked our way between broken branches, upturned mangrove roots and scattered muddy boulders, searching for edible animal life. We were not the only such opportunists: a mongoose accompanied us at a discreet distance, delicately weaving its way between shallow pools and still-draining rivulets of muddy sea water.

She looked almost pretty that afternoon, her long dark hair falling forward as she searched purposefully among the slimy debris, the hem of her kaftan dress soaking and spattered with mud. She had certainly been difficult to supervise, but I had usually managed to squeeze out a few encouraging remarks at the end of her neatly-written essays, which were always idiosyncratic. I remembered how she had mixed up the Statute of Labourers of 1351 with the liability of poll tax of 1381 in her essay on the Peasants' Revolt. What a pity that she was becoming so bad-tempered. Yet she was still the liveliest one in the party and seemed to have taken command in the aftermath of the tidal deluge and the terrible events of the night before.

We had a busy afternoon, splashing about after an amazing assortment of wriggling and thrashing marine organisms. I was particularly wary of the black and yellow sea-snakes, a yard long and poisonous, which were writhing in murky pools. We decided to avoid some fish that inflated themselves like thorny footballs, and anything with sinister-looking spines or fins, like violently coloured Japanese fans. It took all my powers of persuasion to prevent my companion from engaging in mortal combat with what looked like a purple Moray Eel. We eventually accumulated a pile of more innocuous specimens, which she vigorously clubbed to death with a lump of coral. She threaded them, with the aid of Oakley's knife (which still made me shudder just to look at it), along a straight mangrove branch that we shouldered to carry up to the camp. On the way back we came across the sodden photograph of Prince Charles and Princess Diana which had been pinned up inside the rickety cabin of the boat.

It was dusk as we climbed up the rocky path, tired and dirty. The trees were black silhouettes against the lemon and gold of the western sky. We could see the glow of the paraffin lamp and the smoky flickering of the fire. The others had revived enough to prepare the last of the packet soup and were inexpertly frying some of the fish fillets. Oakley had burned himself with hot fat and was cross.

After supper, we sat in the lee of the fire, choking on the acrid smoke, to drive off mosquitoes. Oakley had made a remarkable recovery, but remained despondent. It was then that he admitted that I was probably right – we were on the wrong island.

12

The aftermath was terrible. Our hill was an island in a sea of devastation. The familiar mangroves were gone, and my sanctuary of the night before; no palm stood for more than a mile to east or west and great muddy pools had formed in the shallow boulder-strewn valley behind the hill. The sand had been scoured from the western beach and pushed with broken palm trees like matchsticks against the mountain slopes. Everywhere there were scattered rocks, avalanches of sticky mud and great stretches of torn, red soil. Only the eastern beach was still recognizable, but the dark shape was no longer there. The sea had taken back the Mara.

The following morning revealed fresh miseries. The filleted fish which Doris had laid out to dry had disappeared, stolen in the night by God knows what scavengers. Worse, I discovered the reason for Oakley's hysterical outburst at the break-up of the boat, when I had been so calm and collected. Far from being empty, as I had supposed, most of our dry stores had been on *Bounty II*. Oakley had, only the day before, lugged them back. Not that there was much to lug; only a few pounds of rice, some raisins, half a sack of flour and about four weeks' supply of porridge oats. Oakley had been driven to distraction by hordes of tiny ants which crept through invisible cracks in the metal drums that we had brought precisely for protection against such attack. As it was, all that stood between us and starvation were six cans of corned beef, a few tea bags and enough oats to make one saucepan of porridge. These, Doris decreed, would remain in her charge until we were at death's door – which, as far as I could see, might not be far away.

It had been an astonishing reversal in our fortunes. One day there was the prospect of a thousand pounds of animal flesh and the assurance of our modest stores; on the next it had been snatched away leaving us with a few scraps of food in the midst of a muddy wilderness.

Our difficulties were compounded by the scarcity of the plants and animals with which we had augmented our dwindling provisions. Few birds now appeared within range of Doris's catapult and no fish came to our hooks. Coconuts had been swept from the broken palms and were nowhere to be found. The stretch of dark soil in which we had rooted for De Freville's parsnips had been completely washed away. The shattered shore was abandoned by molluscs and crustaceans alike and the occasional stranded specimens soon rotted in the tropic heat.

Even the drawing of our daily water supply became an exhausting slippery scramble over mud slides, tree trunks and sandy screes. That was the reason why, two days after the deluge, we moved our camp for the third and last time.

It took three journeys to carry the gear up to the watering place in the gorge cut into the steep mountain slope. Doris did the packing. She stacked our precious morsels into a cardboard container and dumped it at my feet as I was shouldering a rucksack. I picked up the box and tottered off followed by Oakley carrying his scientific things; De Freville brought up the rear with a bulging kitbag balanced on top of his rucksack. His long face was puffy and faintly yellowed. He looked like an outraged dromedary as he grumbled about the heat, and his sandfly-tormented midriff.

We had an uncomfortable scramble up to the watering place. Our usual path had been blocked by a landslide and we were forced to straggle along the shore (where Oakley had murdered the leatherback) before turning to climb to our final refuge. Oddly, the contours of that beach were as they had been when the Mara had come ashore. De Freville said that the depth of the offshore water and the lie of the coral reef must have protected that bit of the shore from the full force of the tidal waves.

It was while he was holding forth that the significance of the strange undisturbed beach occurred to me. The leatherback eggs must still be in the sand. I had wanted to see them hatch, but to hell with that – those eggs would keep us alive for days. There must have been more than a hundred of them, possibly a hundred and twenty, maybe even a hundred and fifty. Two eggs a day each should be enough for bare subsistence and that would mean we could hang on for another month. We could always let one hatch and see that its occupant got back to the sea. The only problem would be to find the nest, for although the eastern beach had escaped the full force of the tidal waves its surface had been swept clean and there was no sign of the loose sand which the creature had flung about after burying its eggs.

I put down the cardboard box on the wet sand and slipped off my rucksack. It was going to be difficult, but we were going to find those eggs, I was convinced of that. De Freville reckoned that we were too far to the west, judging from a lava outcrop at the edge of the lagoon which he remembered as being more or less in line with the nest. The leatherback had stopped twenty to thirty yards above the high-tide line – that would help to pinpoint her nest.

While Oakley and I resumed the trek, De Freville strode down the beach to mark a cross in the sand where he thought the eggs were buried. We would come back later and dig them up, he said when he caught up with us. Oakley plodded on in silence. I suspected that he was still feeling pretty sheepish about the butchering of the turtle, which (I had the uneasy feeling) was in some way the cause of our troubles. Anyway, I certainly had no desire to talk to Oakley. For all the good the slaughter had done, the animal could still have been swimming far out to sea.

We dumped our gear at the foot of a fern-smothered cliff close to where the stream burst down from our watering pool. It was unbearably hot. I splashed my face and chest in the cool torrent before following De Freville and Oakley back the way we had come.

It was late in the afternoon before we piled the last of our belongings at the foot of the ferny cliff. We were foolish to have wasted so much of our energy in humping about what was now so much useless junk. It was force of habit, I suppose, and we had still not realized the full extent of our disaster.

Doris used some of our precious paraffin to boil a saucepan of water for a tasteless, straw-coloured infusion from two dried-out tea bags.

We were too tired to put up the tents and just rolled into our sleeping bags on damp stony ground in the gathering dusk. The smell was quite different from our breezy hilltop: musky and humid with a sickly suggestion of decay. There was a constant commotion of falling water.

I was worn out but restless, and sleep would not come.

Hunger pangs tormented me and sharp stones pressed against my sleeping bag. I thought of Molly cooking bacon and eggs in a sunlit kitchen, of soft beds and of kippers on Sunday mornings, and then must have dozed fitfully only to awaken in bright moonlight. De Freville was mumbling in his sleep; Oakley was tossing and turning behind me. Only Doris was tranquil: I could hear her gentle breathing close to my face. I turned, dozed and then woke again. The moonlight picked out every leaf and stone, even the moss on a rock six feet above. My head was aching and my mouth seemed filled with acid. An owl hooting and I noticed that Oakley's sleeping bag lay flat and empty at my side. I covered my eyes with a hand and slept

Doris's raucous shouting dragged me back into consciousness. It was past dawn and the humid air was already warm. I took some seconds to realize that Doris's wrath was directed against me. She was standing, hands on hips, glaring down and tossing her dark hair back in her agitation.

'Doc, what in *hell* did you do with the corned beef?'

'Corned beef?'

'Yeah, the cans of corned beef. *You* brought them up in the box – the cardboard box – *I* gave it to you!'

'Aren't they still there?'

'No they're damned well *not* – you . . . you . . . yo-yo!' Doris stamped her foot in vexation. 'There were six of them – and there are *none* there now.'

'Oh Christ.' It was too much to bear and I put my head in my hands.

'You put the box on the wet sand, Dr Yeo,' the awakened De Freville joined in. 'If the cardboard got wet, the tins could have fallen through.'

I looked up to see the young man gazing at me anxiously. His long face was still grimy except where the perspiration had cut through the dirt of the past few days.

'Is there a hole in the box?' Oakley sat up stretching and yawning. His ginger hair stood out straight from his head as it had when he'd killed the leatherback.

'Not much of one,' Doris replied. 'But you could get a can through one of the corners – which is soaking.' She glared at me accusingly.

'Well, there's no point in arguing about it,' De Freville said. 'We shall just have to find those tins and the leatherback eggs. And we'd better be quick about it before we get too weak to fend for ourselves.'

'OK,' said Doris, 'I'll look for those cans – I know which way you came up here – and you, Doc, can lead the search for the turtle eggs. After all, it was your idea.'

With that, Ms Lakowski stalked off on her quest for the lost corned beef. There was clearly going to be no breakfast – there was nothing to cook. I felt a terrible guilt about those lost tins. Yet it was hard to believe that I had dropped them: I would have heard them fall or felt them hit my legs, for I had held the box in front of me.

Oakley was surprisingly magnanimous about this latest reversal in our fortunes; it was De Freville who kept on and on about when, how and where the damned tins could have fallen through the damp corner of the cardboard box.

Poor De Freville was suffering acutely from lack of food. He had passed well beyond mere feelings of emptiness and was experiencing sharp, recurring stomach pains which he attempted to assuage by drinking cupful after cupful of water.

My hunger pangs seemed to be less severe, although unpleasant enough with a diffuse gnawing sensation in my lower abdomen. I was more shattered from lack of sleep. Oakley seemed to be bearing up well and trotted down to the beach with surprising vigour for someone who had spent such a restless night.

With some difficulty we found the cross that De Freville had made in the sand to mark the turtle's nest – or at least where he thought that it was. De Freville dug down for a couple of feet or so, pushing the spade into the sand with elaborate care, while Oakley and I burrowed and chopped cautiously away with a trowel and the axe at the edges of an enlarging trench.

It was infernally hot. The sun was directly overhead: its heat flung back from the shimmering sand. There were only wave sounds with the suggestion of distant surf and a scrunching of steel against sand. For two hours we laboured in brazen heat, our movements becoming slow and weaker, then slower still and more feeble. There was no sign of the eggs. My head was throbbing and my hands were blistered from chopping and clawing at crumbling sand.

To my surprise, it was De Freville who cracked first. He flung down his spade and slumped on to the edge of the pit, his hands covering his face. He was silent, but I knew that he was weeping. Oakley continued doggedly worrying away at the sand with the trowel, like a terrier in a badger set, while I stood up and put my hand on De Freville's shoulder. Some of my dislike for Oakley dissolved: he really had behaved very well since the killing of the leatherback. Yet I could not shake off the superstitious conviction that the murder was the cause of our troubles.

It was while I was standing dispirited and exhausted, with my hand on De Freville's shoulder, that I realized another curious thing: once again there were no bird sounds. No Sanderling scuttled along at the tide's edge nor was there the creaking call of terns overhead. Yet, even more peculiar, the surface of the beach was pitted with innumerable holes, perfectly circular, each about half an inch in diameter. They seemed too large to have been gouged by any wading bird that I could think of – certainly by the bills of Golden Plovers or Bar-tailed Godwits. Poor De Freville was obviously too distraught to discuss this ornithological paradox, but I resolved to speak to him about it later. It might help to buck him up.

Despite the heat and De Freville's prostration, Oakley continued stubbornly hacking away. His energy was remarkable. Wearily I picked up the spade and laboured at our untidy excavation, which now measured about twenty feet long and some six or eight feet wide. No one spoke: I was beyond speech. De Freville was still huddled on the ground and Oakley was entirely absorbed with his task. There was no sign of Doris, who evidently had not yet found the corned beef.

It was De Freville who broke the silence.

'You might as well save your energies. We'll not find those eggs.'

Oakley and I continued burrowing.

'Christ, we can't dig up the whole bloody beach . . . and there's another outcrop down there,' De Freville flapped an arm despondently. '*That* could be the one I was thinking of.'

'No, I'm sure it's not,' Oakley retorted briskly. 'This is the place, I'm convinced of it. We've just got to keep on until we find the nest. There's no point in giving up now.'

I was grateful for Oakley's confidence. He was showing real leadership: a quality that I was singularly lacking on that awful beach. My arms were aching dreadfully and the hunger pangs had returned with redoubled intensity.

Worst of all was a terrible weakness. I could hardly lift the spadefuls of sand from the trench. The heat was appalling and I knew that I was not far from collapse.

Oakley put his hand on my shoulder.

'Come on, Yeo, let's take a break. We can at least cool off and quench our thirst.'

My colleague dropped the trowel and strode off in the direction of our inadequate camp. De Freville and I straggled after him. I noticed again the regular holes in the sand, but could not summon the energy to point them out to De Freville. Could they have been made by a Bristle-thighed Curlew, a Whimbrel or even a Wandering Tattler? Surely they wouldn't have made holes like that? Perhaps some sort of burrowing invertebrate had been temporarily unhinged by the full moon. It didn't matter anyway. It seemed very unlikely that I would survive to send in a note about it to one of the bird journals.

We found Doris squatting on the ground when we returned to camp. She did not look up or respond to Oakley's greeting.

I walked over to comfort her. Was she too giving up? She pushed my hand away and glared up in a most unpleasant manner.

'Doc, you stupid old bastard,' she snarled. 'Trust you to lose those cans. How could you have been so stupid . . .' She faltered and put her head in her hands, just as De Freville had done earlier that dreadful morning.

'Now, come on,' Oakley commented. 'There's no point in carrying on like this. It won't do any good at all. We can at least have a nice cool drink.'

'And you can shut up too – you pompous jerk,' Doris retorted.

This was awful. I felt that I had to say something.

'Look, Doris, let's at least keep some vestige . . .'

'Piss off,' retorted Ms Lakowski as she struggled to her feet. 'I'll go and have another look for those goddamned cans.'

With that my undergraduate limped off (she seemed to have something wrong with her right foot) leaving me guilty and more upset than I had been in the whole of my adult life. I remember thinking of the terrible essay which Doris had written on the origins of the Peasants' Revolt.

It was then, in the depths of my despair, that I heard again the strange whistling call which had so baffled me when we had first arrived on the island.

13

We must have sat for more than an hour amidst the humid greenery, dominated by the sound of tumbling water. It seemed a secret, hidden place after the blazing exposure of the beach. No one spoke. I was too tired for utterance and De Freville had flopped on to his sleeping bag, an arm flung across his eyes. Even Oakley showed no inclination to return to the beach. I supposed that he was tactfully waiting for me to recover from Doris's temper. His presence was reassuring. At least one of us was attempting to cope with our terrible predicament.

It was Oakley who broke the gloomy silence.

'How . . . what . . . do you chaps think we should do if . . . if one us should go first?'

'*Do?*' I croaked. 'Do about *what*?'

'And if it comes to that,' De Freville chipped in, without lifting his head from his sleeping bag, 'what do you mean – *go*?'

'Well, you know, if one of us should . . . like – pass on,' Oakley stammered. 'We've got to face up to that possibility. Even if we find the eggs they'll only last for a week or two and there seems precious little else to eat since the tidal wave and we'll be getting weaker all the time.'

Despite the shock that it gave me, Oakley's reasoning impressed me again with the really quite courageous manner in which he seemed to be facing up to our awful prospects. In a strange way it was almost comforting.

'You see,' Oakley continued, 'we ought to be thinking

about what we are going to *do* if the worst happens – to one or other of us. And we should decide without worrying Doris. I know that there are taboos but . . .'

'Taboos?' De Freville was now sitting up, his grubby face puckered as it used to be when he was mystified by one of my more obscure historical expositions. '*Taboos? We just bury . . . whoever it is. Good God, we don't have to worry about taboos – Christ!*'

With that, the lanky undergraduate flopped back on to his sleeping bag and covered his eyes again.

'Yes, but there is a moral question here.' Oakley dropped his voice.

'How do you make that out?' De Freville said, now sitting up again.

'It's simply a matter of proteins.'

'Proteins?' De Freville and I chorused.

'Well, you . . .' Oakley faltered, 'you see, it doesn't do to be too squeamish about these things. I don't think you know, Yeo, but I have long had an interest in voluntary euthanasia and those of us in our group regularly face up to the . . . ultimate human problem.'

'But what has that got to do with proteins?' the still sleepy De Freville squeaked.

'Oh come on,' said Oakley. 'We had better get back to the beach.'

At the time I found it difficult to follow the drift of whatever it was that Oakley was going on about. I hadn't known about his involvement in euthanasia. I'll bet Cecil Fox didn't either: it would be just the sort of thing that he would batten on to.

I was fatigued and light-headed from lack of food. It was strange, I could remember things but couldn't think very clearly.

* * *

Although it was well past noon, the sun still blazed down with undiminished ferocity on the empty shore. It had taken a considerable effort of will for me to follow De Freville (who now seemed more lively) and Oakley back to the site of our labours. The excavation looked tiny on that enormous beach.

I began mutely to dig away once more, while Oakley and De Freville argued about the probable location of the turtle's nest. De Freville maintained that he had been mistaken and that the eggs were most likely to be buried a couple of hundred yards down the beach, opposite to the other lava outcrop. Oakley was adamant that they were where De Freville had said they were in the first place. He became quite heated about it and grabbed the spade from me to make sure that it would not be taken further along the shore.

We worked for a couple of hours, taking turns with the spade while the others pushed the sand away from the diggings, which we slowly enlarged to twice the area by our flagging efforts. We found no turtle eggs.

It was a testimony to Oakley's powers of persuasion that he kept De Freville and me working away at the original site. He certainly would not have got the better of De Freville if that formidable undergraduate had been in full possession of his faculties. As it was, the young man was suffering acutely from starvation pains, lassitude and, like me, was finding it difficult to concentrate adequately or even properly to co-ordinate his digging movements.

Somehow or other we kept at our work until the mountain slopes darkened with purple shadows and wispy clouds were silhouetted against the fading western sky. My hands were blistered and my shoulders stabbed with pain. It took us nearly half an hour to totter up to our mossy refuge. Oakley helped me up the steepest part of the rocky incline.

It was dusk when we stumbled into the camp. Doris was crouched on her sleeping bag. She did not speak. I knew that she had not found the corned beef. It was troubling to see Doris so silent, subdued – and accusing. Yet she had found something: there was a small coconut lying beside her on the sleeping bag.

Doris was very good about the coconut. She cracked it with a single blow of the axe and dribbled the milk carefully into our chipped enamel mugs; then she chopped the nut with great care and considerable accuracy into four equal portions which she handed round with elaborate courtesy.

She served me last. I was squatting on my sleeping bag savouring the coconut milk nectar which was cooling my ulcerating mouth. Doris paused as she put the fibrous segment into my hand.

'Have you stashed those cans someplace, Doc?'

I could not see her face clearly in the failing light, but sensed anxiety in an unfamiliar catch in her voice.

'Well, have you?' Doris persisted. 'Because if you have . . .'

It took me a couple of seconds, in my hunger-befuddled state, to realize what Doris meant. I was so appalled that I could only open and close my mouth like a demented parrot fish.

Without speaking, Doris lifted my free hand and pressed something hard and metallic into the palm. It was one of the small metal keys which are used for opening corned-beef tins.

'I found *this* on the edge of the thorn bushes near those piles of loose rocks. Do you know how it got there?'

Doris glared down at me: her rage seemed tangible in the damp gloom.

'Leave off, Doris,' De Freville squeaked.

'Shut up, Donald, you dickhead.' Doris flicked her skirt irritably. 'We've got to locate those cans, even if we've . . .'

'All right, all right.' Oakley pulled himself to his feet. 'There's absolutely *no* point in all this.'

Oakley propelled Doris back to her sleeping bag. His bottom wobbled with self-importance. I noticed how skinny Doris's wrists had become.

We gnawed miserably away at Doris's coconut. It was generous of her to have given me a piece if she really believed that I had pinched the bully beef. Yet I felt helpless, old and quite unable to cope with Doris's latest outburst. My hunger pangs were returning, as abdominal cramps spread upwards to my shoulders, and I was desperately tired. I dozed fitfully, dreaming of food-laden tables stretching away to infinity in lush English meadows. My mother, young and beautiful as I remembered her as a child, was offering me fruit cake and cups of steaming cocoa which dissolved as soon as I reached for them.

I drifted into consciousness. There was the familiar moonlight scene. De Freville and Doris were lying on their sleeping bags: she was dozing with her back towards me; he on his back with an arm shielding his eyes. My arm had pins and needles and my shoulders were aching. A faint mist obscured the tumbling stream. I could see the buckles on De Freville's rucksack glistening in the soft light and Oakley's sleeping bag empty on the damp rock as I slid into a dream of pink blancmange and freshly-laundered sheets.

It was dawn when I awoke again from restless, troubled

sleep. The sky was already flooding with gold and crimson. I closed my eyes to blot out reality with thoughts of Molly cooking shepherd's pie and apple crumble and of the High Table, candlelit, with nuts and brandy at the Fellows' Christmas Dinner. But that had been the cause of my troubles, with Cecil Fox plotting to get me here with De Freville and Doris. He must have guessed that something like this would happen.

I groaned and turned again to ease the discomfort of my tortured back. Oakley's sleeping bag had gone. He must have hung it up as he had the day before and gone off to scout for food. It was comforting that he, at least, was staying level-headed.

Doris was the next to waken. She stumbled out of her warm cocoon, and made straight for the miniature waterfall that was our shower and drinking fountain. I turned over as she sloshed about at her ablutions and returned to my private misery.

'Where's he gone then?'

Doris was standing over me. Her voice was harsh and still belligerent, as though I was somehow responsible now for the disappearance of Oakley's sleeping bag.

'Gone?'

'Yeah. When did he take off?'

I sat up; De Freville stirred, on the verge of consciousness.

'He hasn't taken off as far as I know,' I replied as civilly as I could. 'He must have hung his sleeping bag up to dry and gone somewhere.'

'I'll say he's gone! I can't see his bag *or* his rucksack *or* the bucket, if it comes to that. And the spade has gone missing as well – the *asshole*. It was *him* who hijacked the corned beef,' Doris concluded, ungrammatically.

138

She knelt down and put her hand on my arm.

'Gee, I'm sorry, Doc – I really thought it was you. It seemed . . .' Doris faltered and squeezed my arm in her agitation. 'I'll make it up to you, I *really* will. You can have another cuddle if you like.'

'Cuddle?'

'Yeah, like you did the other night . . .'

'Now look here, Doris . . .' I was acutely conscious that De Freville was sitting up, dishevelled and bleary-eyed, but obviously aware of what was going on.

'Christ,' he shouted.

'Now look here, De Freville . . .' I stammered.

'He's got the eggs. He's got the bloody eggs.' De Freville groaned. 'That's what all those holes were doing in the sand. I *thought* they were too big for godwits and they couldn't have been made by a whimbrel. Why didn't I think of that? He must have found them by poking about with a stick during the night. That's why he kept us digging away at what I was sure was the wrong place!'

De Freville picked up his binoculars, scrambled out of his sleeping bag and walked slowly down the rocky incline to get a better view of the beach. He was back in five minutes with the news that there was a second, smaller excavation about two hundred yards away from the one on which we had laboured the day before. There was no sign of Oakley.

I suppose that we should have hunted for him. There would have been footprints in the sand. Perhaps we could have persuaded him to rejoin us or, failing that, have taken the food by brute force. But we were weakened by days of starvation and shocked by the turn of events.

Doris was the first to recover. She started to tidy the camp as she always did at that time of day. Her rage had subsided; she seemed close to tears. Then De Freville stood up, removed his shirt and went to sluice himself in the cataract which tumbled down from the mountain slopes. It was the first time that he had washed since the killing of the Mara. I stayed in my sleeping bag. My hunger pains were less intense, but I felt dizzy and light-headed. Yet I had to think what we should do. De Freville and Doris were my responsibility now.

It was strange that no one had come to look for us. We had not seen a ship or boat since we had been on the island: there was only the distant sound of the aeroplane which De Freville claimed to have heard. Our position was now worse than ever. At least our previous camp had been visible from the sea. Now we were hidden, perched up in our mountainside grotto. No one would know where we were, even if a boat landed on the island, and how would we see even if a boat approached? We would have to set a watch where we could look out to sea. And we would have to keep our eyes open for Oakley. How would he get his water, I wondered? If he did not find it somewhere else, he would have to come here. He had the food but we guarded the water. Perhaps we could overpower him or follow him to wherever he was hiding and then deal with him. That would be easier. If he tried to light a fire we would see the smoke. The trouble was that he would be well nourished. But we had the axe if it ever came to a fight, and there were three of us. We had better find out exactly what he *had* taken. It would be a lot for him to haul in one go. He might be still close at hand if he was going to move it in stages.

Then another thought: those mynah birds which had attached themselves to us at the other camp – according to Hartlaub they were only found close to human dwellings. So where had they come from? They would hardly have flown from another island. And there was that business with Doris about the footprints. Why had she been so upset and made De Freville promise not to tell Oakley and me about them? Was it just that she was pregnant, as De Freville believed? Good God – *just* pregnant – that would be the last straw.

'Well Doc, what are we going to do?'

I turned to find Doris looking down at me. De Freville was towelling himself in the background. At least he was cleaner, but I was shocked at his protruding ribs, his gaunt face and the dark lines under his eyes.

Wearily I pushed myself on to my feet and stood up. My back was aching dreadfully and I noticed that my hands were trembling. The sun was now overhead, but I felt strangely cold inside – like ice in warm water.

'Come on,' I heard myself saying. 'We'll take it in turns.'

I was not quite sure what we were going to take turns doing, but Doris and De Freville nodded in agreement.

'De Freville and I will scout round,' I continued vaguely. 'We must find something to eat and we *might* find where Oakley is hiding.'

My undergraduates nodded again.

'And you stay here, Doris. Just in case Oakley comes back for water – or anything else.'

We picked our way slowly down to the shore in the sticky heat. De Freville was chewing a stem of grass from the bunch that he had stuffed into his pocket. He had topped himself up with stream water which, he said, kept his stomach stretched although, like me, his hunger pains and abdominal cramps were abating. My main difficulty at this time was simply one of mental concentration – or, rather, lack of it. I could now think with remarkable clarity, but then would lose my train of thought and switch to a quite different topic.

It was just such a bout of lucidity that led me to talk to De Freville, as we walked down to the beach, about the likely whereabouts of the bird which bore his name and which was the primary reason for his coming to the islands. He showed surprisingly little interest in my idea that if *Petrodroma defrevillei* was like *Petrodroma arminjoniana heraldica* then there could still be fledglings around – even so late in the season – and that we would find them by cutting our way upwards and following the course of our stream into the misty highlands. Neither was he particularly impressed with my scheme for pulling a fast one on Oakley by finding some of his peculiar insects and using them to bargain for a few turtle eggs or even a tin of bully beef.

De Freville seemed to have difficulty in following the drift of my argument, for I had to keep repeating myself to get through to him. We also had a sharp difference of opinion concerning the topography of the island. De Freville maintained that the lava promontory on which I had caught the shark was a mile or more to the right, while I knew very well that it was only a matter of a few hundred yards away.

It took us more than half an hour to get to the promontory, largely because De Freville insisted on a quite unnecessary detour to avoid a channel that had been driven through the sand by the tidal waves and which I am sure we could have waded without difficulty. We spent a long time in fruitless pursuit of some elusive fiddler crabs; a sad remnant of the nimble horde from before the deluge. Again, no fish came to our hooks, which we were unable to bait properly, so great had been the destruction of crab, mollusc and worm on that broken shore.

We started back, empty-handed, in awful midday heat.

Once more we had squandered our dwindling bodily resources for no benefit whatsoever. Poor De Freville had scooped up a few mouthfuls of sea water and was now feeling sick. Yet it was probably a sensible thing to do: it would at least top up his body salts in the face of the aqueous onslaught to which he was subjecting his kidneys just to keep his stomach full.

There was no sign of Oakley, only the dazzling beach, the thorny ramparts of the bush, tangled with the debris of the deluge, and the empty shore washed by the rising tide. A solitary Swamp Harrier hung in the hot air, in equally hopeless search for prey.

Slowly we retraced our steps. My legs ached, my head was throbbing and I was frightened. We could not last much longer. I knew that. Maybe only a few days, perhaps a week or two. How had I got into such a mess? If Cecil Fox had plotted my undoing by sending me off with Oakley, then he had succeeded beyond what must have been his wildest hopes.

I wondered again whether the hateful Fox had known about Oakley's macabre interest. He might have wheedled it out of Muriel Oakley. Odd that Oakley had never told me about it. He had said that we should not be squeamish. And what was that stuff about taboos and proteins?

Christ, it was obvious. Why hadn't I realized it? He was going to *eat Doris*. A plastic bag over the head in our exhausted condition would bring a swift end, and more protein for Oakley. In my disconnected flash of insight it was crystal clear. Yet I could not bring myself to tell De Freville and we laboured on in silence.

We skirted the deepening channel, which now really was uncrossable, straggled past the open pit from which Oakley had taken the turtle eggs, and climbed wearily upwards beside the tumbling stream towards the leafy platform in the rock that was our last refuge in that dreadful paradise. A large purple butterfly pirouetted in the humid air, but there was no other sign of life, for Doris was nowhere to be seen.

It was then that I told De Freville of my fears.

14

It was difficult to persuade De Freville that a Fellow of the College might be tempted to eat an undergraduate. Yet I noticed that he was very relieved when Doris reappeared some half an hour after our return to camp. She squeezed out from dense vegetation at the stream's edge. Like us, she was empty-handed and very scratched.

Doris, it transpired, had been anxious after we had gone.

'It was kinda spooky round here after you guys took off. I felt like there was someone looking at me *all the time*. So I tried to squeeze along the edge of the stream to find something we could eat.'

Odd that she too felt she was being watched, not, apparently, by that 'asshole', because the feeling had started before Oakley had 'taken off'.

Ever since we landed I had entertained the eerie conviction that we were not alone on the island. At first it was a vague feeling: as a solitary climber might suspect that there is someone on the other side of the mountain. However, as the days passed the sensation intensified. It had nothing to do with mynah birds or mysterious footprints, I was convinced of that.

The feeling grew stronger still after we moved up to the watering place. It was not so much the sensation of being watched, such as Doris experienced, but a sense almost of companionship, of the closeness of another human being; it was not frightening as was the thought of Oakley lurking in gathering dusk or peering in dappled sunlight from the safety of the tangled bush. Whatever it was seemed closer after the spasms of lucidity, when I was almost in a waking dream. It also came between bouts of restless, hunger-drawn sleep.

Our need for rest increased as starvation gripped us. I found it difficult to stay awake during the day when I was on my own, but then only slid into a shallow doze. At night I would wake frequently, and then sink into heavy sleep as the early-morning light filtered into our camp.

We crept into our beds at sunset for our third night at the watering place and our fifth day of starvation; De Freville and I were exhausted and, besides, there was nothing else that we could do. Doris had laid our sleeping bags close together on the stony ground and slipped into the middle one after a perfunctory splash at the waterfall.

I drifted in and out of sleep through the moonlit night, no longer troubled by hunger pains, just weak and so very tired. Yet I recall worrying that Doris might go on again about having a cuddle, with De Freville's big ears flapping only a few inches away. I certainly did not *feel* like a cuddle, as Doris had described it – not on that dismal night. But I need not have worried. Doris went out like a light, as she had in those glorious days of food in our cosy tent on the hill with the comforting sound of distant surf to lull our sleep.

We had decided not to keep watch for Oakley. I would have been unable to remain awake anyway and there seemed little chance of catching him. Looking back, I can see that we were slipping into a dangerous apathy and had already passed the point at which we could properly fend for ourselves. Strangely, I was not unhappy or, despite my normally timid nature, particularly frightened. In fact I remember unfamiliar feelings of contentment from that time: feelings which were marred only by the difficulty of holding sensible conversations with De Freville, who seemed quite unable to grasp what I was saying during moments of surprising clarity of thought.

I began to appreciate the psychological effects of fasting on mystical experience and, evidently, on superstition, for I was now wholly convinced that our troubles sprang directly from the murder of the Mara. Yet in my confused state it was difficult to understand why the perpetrator of the crime should be so well nourished while we drifted inexorably towards death. I could only conclude that a more protracted and nastier fate awaited him.

While I was pondering these mysteries, and deliberately trying not to over-dramatize our plight, I saw the figure for the first time, standing near the waterfall. I had drifted from a restless dream of bread and butter pudding into the unreality of the moonlit scene. Doris was snoring at my back; I could not tell what De Freville was doing. The noise of tumbling water seemed distant and oddly subdued. I did not move, but just blinked my eyes and stared at the edge of the waterfall.

The figure was too tall for Oakley: its face was indistinct, the hair falling on to the shoulders of a purplish, flowing garment. Then the sound of falling water increased and the shape faded into the night mist which shrouded the foot of the falls as I slid into gentle sleep until sunlight warmed my face.

That morning De Freville started his hymn singing. It was dreadful: I was surprised that he could remember the words of so many of them, but he had been a choirboy at Tetbury (before the onset of adolescent unbelief) and the shock of his recent experiences seemed to bring total recall. It turned out that De Freville's youthful agnosticism had been overthrown in the night. Like me, he had experienced powerful feelings of closeness to something, which he referred to with dramatic emphasis as the 'Unseen Presence' – hence the hymns.

There had always been something of the parson about De Freville. I noticed it during his first term; before he developed the withering historical erudition which swiftly drove such inconsequential thoughts from my mind. As it was, his parsonical ego stood revealed by our desperate circumstances.

De Freville's liturgical tastes inclined towards the lugubrious, with a strong emphasis on doom.

His favourite was 'Lighten the darkness of our life's long night', closely followed by 'Fierce raged the tempest o'er the deep', which I found particularly harrowing although perhaps not so unnerving as his very idiosyncratic singing of the Nunc Dimittis. (De Freville told me afterwards that he had no recollection of any of these, except 'Nearer my God to Thee'.)

Surprisingly, in view of his previous musical outpourings on the island, he droned in a sad, cracked tenor. He would commence during his morning shower, which got later and later as the days passed, but could burst forth at almost any time of the day, before a final mournful session in his sleeping bag at night.

De Freville was particularly concerned that we should maintain forgiveness for Oakley – and here he ran foul of Doris who was in a remarkably aggressive state of mind.

'If you think I'm going to forgive that *asshole*, you've got another think coming.'

Doris was off on one of her regular forays to try and push her way further up the mountainside. She always came back empty-handed, but was convinced that was where our hopes lay. Yet there was more to it than that – for Doris too felt an unseen presence.

'Don't you guys find it spooky round here? Like someone is *looking* all the time?'

I learned later that the sensation of another presence is almost universal among castaways, even the intrepid Josh Slocum entertained Christopher Columbus's pilot on board the *Spray* and Sir Francis Chichester saw some very strange things on *Gypsy Moth IV*.

I did not tell De Freville about the figure at the waterfall, for I was convinced that it would send him off again: especially if he learned about the flowing garment and long hair. Intuitively, I knew he would say it was Jesus, 'The Light of the World', as Holman Hunt had painted him standing gentle and beautiful in the dark garden. So I held my peace. De Freville's hymn singing was getting me down; I had no intention of giving him an excuse for starting again. In any case, I knew that it was a woman I saw fade into the mist.

The next day I saw her clearly: standing in the shade of a clump of tree ferns which had survived the tidal waves. She seemed young, barely more than twenty years old. Her hair was fair and piled on top of her head. The dress had a full skirt with a high bodice and short puffy sleeves. She moved her head, almost as though seeking my approval, then stepped into deeper shadows and was gone.

I could not recall any woman who looked like that. Yet, somehow, she seemed familiar – and very reassuring. Her costume might have been a ball gown – she seemed happy enough for that – it could have been Elizabethan, for all I could tell. She had changed her hair. I suppose that it would be modern to wear it up.

Whoever she was, I adored her, even though I knew that she was intangible.

I saw her often after our second meeting. I could never

149

see her face clearly, but she told me that she would come for me and it would be on the thirteenth day. The trouble was that I could not remember the thirteenth day after *what*. Yet her promise gave me a certain hope – we just had to wait and we would be found.

My contentment and optimism infuriated Doris: De Freville and I were frequently requested to move our asses. This became progressively difficult, in the sense that Doris intended, because I was drowsy for much of the time, and tired quickly, while De Freville was often preoccupied and, infuriatingly, seemed unable to concentrate properly when I had one of my uncharacteristic bouts of mental gymnastics. I could not even tempt him with speculation of the origins of Lollardy – a topic on which I felt I could now grapple with him on more equal terms. It just set him off on the 23rd Psalm. Neither could I stimulate his interest in *Petrodroma defrevillei*. In fact, he retorted with quite unnecessary profanity when I mentioned the petrel and then launched into a diatribe about 'the children of Mordoch' (I am sure that De Freville made them up: he used to invent things in supervision classes).

De Freville was lethargic for much of the time, content to sprawl on his sleeping bag, picking at his scabs, and maunder on like a half-baked curate; Doris on the other hand had surprising energy. So much that I wondered whether she too might have a cache somewhere in the undergrowth.

Doris was obsessed with the thought of Oakley's cornucopia. She even tried to get De Freville to work out the likely rate of development of turtle embryos in the hope that one of them might grow sufficiently to lodge in my former colleague's throat while he enjoyed a lightly-boiled egg somewhere up the island.

It was odd that there was no sign of Oakley – no footprint, eggshell or plume of smoke. Not that we ventured far from our leafy hideout. Doris saw to that: we were going to cut a way up beside that stream if it was the 'last damned thing' we did. As far as I could see that was exactly what it was going to be.

Doris's energy came in short bursts and for much of the time she too would loll about on her sleeping bag. We talked about many things during those hot, listless hours; about ice cream and regattas; lardy cakes and evolution. De Freville even got round to Doris's 'condition'. He came straight out with it. Doris's response was spectacular.

'Wadya mean – you schmuck?' Doris was fairly gibbering. Her hunger-drawn face was a livid contortion, like a Japanese war mask. I would not have been surprised if flames had flickered from her nostrils.

'Seven months *gone*?' she bawled. 'Gone from *when* – and with *who*!'

De Freville stuttered on about Oakley and the Fellows' Christmas Dinner and how she had slept in College that night and how I had told him about it and that was more than seven months ago

'You stupid assholes!'

Doris was hopping about in the extremity of her rage. It was the first time that I had seen anyone doing that. She really was jumping up and down.

She caught me in one of my 'up' moods, but, again, I was depressed by her limited anal imagery. Like everything else nowadays, cursing was a mere shadow of former glories. If Doris had succeeded in convincing us about her 'condition', she had certainly not finished with De Freville and me.

151

'Bird droppings, indeed,' she shrieked. 'And what in hell *were* you doing with my tissue paper?'

Her rage washed harmlessy over me. My hazy contentment was hardly dented by Doris's vituperation. De Freville was also unmoved. He continued worrying away at some septic spots which had abruptly appeared that morning, on his left ankle. I certainly had no intention of apologizing to Doris.

Our lack of response diverted Doris's rage, for she stamped off to initiate, albeit unwittingly, one of the most remarkable series of events in the history of ornithology.

15

It was a testimony to Doris's determination that she should have continued in her attempt to force a way up the precipitous, wooded mountainside above us. By this time De Freville and I had abandoned all pretence: we hardly strayed from our encampment and spent most of the daylight hours dozing or just flopped out on our sleeping bags. To me this was an entirely sensible thing to do. After all, the lady had said that we would be saved on the 'thirteenth day'. Not that I told De Freville this, for I knew that he would carry on about Jezebels and 'the children of Mordoch' and goodness knows what else.

We were all shockingly skinny and De Freville seemed to be coming out in spots on all exposed surfaces. Only Doris exhibited any determination. She certainly showed this when she pushed her way between the tangle of vegetation next to our waterfall, paused to raise the middle finger of her right hand to a vertical position, and then disappeared from sight: a final defiant gesture of contempt at two pathetic males.

De Freville and I lolled on our sleeping bags. It was well past midday, but my drowsiness had returned and there seemed little point in Doris's frantic bursts of activity if we were to be rescued with seven days.

It was steamingly hot: a secret sort of afternoon. The insect hum was barely audible; even the falling water seemed strangely distant, a subdued commotion merging with the throbbing pulse within my head. De Freville dozed while I slipped into a sick trance, sitting with my back pressed against the damp rock and my nostrils feeling as if they had been rinsed with acid.

I suppose that I might have been nearing the end. Yet I was quite content and felt more than ever the comfort of my lady in the purple dress. I even revived a little as the shadows lengthened.

De Freville stirred at dusk, roused no doubt by a sudden cooling breeze, magically funnelled up from the sea.

I spoke to De Freville. He turned his head towards me, nodded and closed his eyes again.

It was then that I saw the black figure silhouetted against the darkening sky.

His hair stood wildly from his head as it had when he had killed the turtle. In his right hand he held something that I knew was a plastic bag. Oakley stood there for half a minute that seemed like eternity and then he was gone.

I had not moved a muscle, nor did I for another half a minute before leaning across to prod weakly at De Freville's haunch with the handle of the frying pan which had inexplicably found its way to my bedside.

'De Freville,' I hissed. 'It's him, I've seen him.'

'What?'

'I saw him.'

'Who?'

'Oakley!'

'The *asshole*.'

'Yeah.'

'Christ.'

I hardly knew what to make of De Freville's ejaculation in his present state of mind: I feared yet another religious outburst. But he merely picked up the torch which he always kept beside his sleeping bag and shone it wildly around the grotto.

Then several things happened in rapid succession.

A dark shape fluttered into the torchlight, spiralled down like a black shuttlecock and landed on De Freville's head, just as Doris stepped out from the enveloping gloom. With a swift swinging movement she raised her catapult and let fly. William Tell could not have done better: the poor creature tumbled from De Freville's cranium – flapping horribly – black against the rusty soil. Doris grabbed the frying pan and whacked at the struggling bird, obliterating its head with a ghastly crunch. Then she flung down the frying pan, snatched up the corpse and dropped it into De Freville's lap.

'Hi Donald – there's some chow.'

So saying, she turned to the edge of the darkness and retrieved another feathered bundle and tossed it in my direction.

'. . . and yours, Doc.'

In my debilitated condition it took several seconds for me to identify *what* Doris had thrown on to the ground. It was certainly a duck, of medium size, say, about a foot and a half from bill to tail, with dark-brown upper parts, a white throat patch and ungainly legs with enormous pinkish feet.

After a while, I realized what it was.

'De Freville,' I croaked; I found my skinny, starved hands were shaking. 'It's *Dendrocygna . . . Dendrocygna arcuata . . . Dendrocygna arcuata* Horsfield – if I'm not mistaken.'

But I knew that I was not. It was a Wandering Whistling Duck, according to Hartlaub, extinct in the archipelago. *What* a find and *what* a way for an ornithologist to go – like Sir Galahad finding the holy grail. I thought of the mysterious calls I had heard, like a melodious bosun's pipe. I might never write this up, but by God what a way to go!

It was odd that I should have thought of my death with such certainty, but I felt then that it was inevitable. The mental turmoil of discovery had somehow driven away the confidence of rescue promised by the lady in the purple dress.

I started to weep, as I thought of Molly and how she would never know of our discovery. It was then, in the midst of my own misery, that I saw that De Freville was also in tears. I groped for his hand and pulled him towards me.

'It's got double white wing bars,' De Freville sobbed through his tears.

He dropped the blood-stained corpse on to the ground and I looked down at the first specimen of *Petrodroma defrevillei* knowingly seen by human eyes for nearly a century.

De Freville clung to me in a storm of emotion. I was not exactly sure of its origin – ornithological elation, overpowering fear or extreme frustration – but there was no doubt as to its intensity.

'What is this . . . what is this?' Doris bawled. 'Cut it out, you guys.' Doris neatly decapitated the whistling duck with two blows of the axe and, without further ado, began to pluck away at the brown feathers which fluttered in the torchlight and settled around her like delicate autumn leaves.

Her industry seemed to calm her.

'Come on, Doc, get a fire going and *you*, Donald, can keep your eyes skinned for the asshole. He might try some kind of snatch job when he discovers we're having supper. He'll see the fire for sure.'

Doris had the duck plucked within minutes and then

started on *Petrodroma defrevillei*. Whan it had been reduced to nakedness she chopped off the legs of duck and petrel, plastered the corpses with mud from the pool edge and pushed them into the blaze which, fortunately, I had been able to coax from what was to have been our signal fire.

We sat staring at the flames. I was exhausted by the effort of lighting that fire, but, strangely, was not at all excited by the prospect of food after so many hungry days. This may have been because I was far gone in the apathy of starvation, but I think it was more the outrageous improbability of what Doris had done. It was like burning the *Mona Lisa* to make toast or smashing the Elgin marbles for a rockery.

De Freville had recovered sufficiently to start on again about the children of Mordoch and the miracle which had brought the family petrel fluttering on to his head. It dawned on me that he was not overpowered by ornithological guilt, as I was. Far from it, his emotions were stirred in quite another way: by thoughts of mysterious forces which had brought our bizarre supper to us in such a strange and timely manner.

I did not awake until after dawn the next morning. It had been a terrible night. My nervous stomach had played up again: I vomited three times before midnight (I think it was De Freville's petrel that did it) and, consequently, derived no nutritional benefit from Doris's historic slaughter. Fortunately, Doris and De Freville managed to hold down the half-raw, half-burnt flesh, and he seemed much revived when he struggled from his sleeping bag that morning, the thirteenth since the tidal wave.

I had not seen De Freville in such a lively state for many days. Doris, too, was in high feather – at least by our debilitated standards. It turned out that she had succeeded in cutting her way up to a largish lake which was evidently the source of our cataract and of the whistling duck. She had apparently explained this to me on the previous evening, but such was my difficulty in understanding what was happening for much of the time, together with the ornithological excitement, that I had failed to grasp it.

There was no question of my accompanying them up to the lake that morning. I felt far too weak and, as I could tell from their anxious looks, appeared to them to be in a pretty bad way. Doris at least was very tactful about it and said that it would be best if I stayed to guard the camp and fend off Oakley should he reappear. They would be taking the axe with them, she explained, but I could use the frying pan to lash out at my colleague if he made a nuisance of himself.

So it was that they left me, lying in my sleeping bag on the stony ground, with the frying pan close to hand in case of emergency.

In my drowsy state I was finding it difficult to concentrate on anything for long or to distinguish dream from reality. Doris had left a mug of cool stream water beside me on the ground. It was just as I propped myself up on one elbow to take a sip that I saw the purple figure coming towards me from the waterfall. She came closer than she had ever done before. I could still not see her face properly, until she bent over me. Then her features came into focus, with every detail sharply defined: an oval, sallow face with close-set eyes and pouting piranha lips – Muriel Oakley.

The terrible shock of recognition set off one of my occasional bouts of unhealthy mental energy. Even so, I can now only recall fragments of what Muriel told me as

158

I lay shivering, despite the humid heat. Yet I am convinced (for I remember feeling very relieved at the time) that she did not mention the encounter at 27 Hillingdon Drive. Instead, she spoke of Cecil Fox and how he had secured my undoing by plotting for me to come to the islands. It was something to do with the carpet committee, she said. Cecil Fox knew that I would come to grief left to my own devices on a desert island and he had thrown in the Lakowski girl for good measure. None of us knew the danger that my undergraduate had brought with her, Muriel hissed, her face coming closer and closer to mine; neither did I know of what Derek was capable (she'd not shown me *those pictures* in his bedroom) and as for De Freville – well, he was potty.

I could smell furniture polish and the scent of hyacinths, strangely evil in the humid air, and then the foetid waft of her breath on my face. Her eyes were glittering and her lips immobile, like a ventriloquist's, as she rambled on about the killing of the Mara that had brought the punishment from the sea; how this was the place for the death of those who attempted adultery and how Derek would kill again, but not with a knife. This was the thirteenth day, she whispered in silvery tones, and she had come, as she had promised, and there was no hope.

'Get away, you bitch,' I croaked and shut my eyes.

The smell of hyacinths filled my nostrils and then subsided. When I opened my eyes she had gone.

I realize now the strange tricks that starvation and solitude can play with the human mind.

Yet for me – a skinny, frightened heap of bones – cowering in my sleeping bag on the red, stony ground, this was awful reality. There was no hope and I would die. I thought of Molly, young and pretty, as she had been

159

on our honeymoon, with the sunlight glinting through her fair hair on a Devon beach, and of innumerable futile wranglings with De Freville on the origins of Lollardy and the Peasants' Revolt.

I must have drifted into unconsciousness for I can remember nothing more until the sun was high overhead, shining directly down into our grotto. My shoulders were aching dreadfully and I shifted in the hot sleeping bag.

Suddenly I saw Oakley standing as he had before, looking down at me sprawled at his feet. I opened and shut my parched mouth, then swallowed some water from the mug and eventually managed to speak.

'Did Muriel send you?'

Oakley remained silent.

'Did she?' There was still no answer.

'Why do you come here?' I persisted, every word a monstrous effort. 'You've got the eggs, why bother now . . . ?'

Oakley shifted uneasily and scratched a still plump buttock.

'They've been eaten – mostly. Some blasted beatles keep getting into them.'

His voice was husky and oddly hesitant as though he had carefully to test each word.

'Why did you take them, Oakley?' I blurted out in a hoarse whisper. 'We would have shared . . .'

'. . . and none of us would have survived. At least this way I'm in better shape to continue my work – and that's bigger than all of us.'

Oakley crouched down on his haunches, his grubby face animated, cunning glinting in his eyes.

'Look, Yo-Yo,' he said. 'I know – I tell you that I *know* – something that's going to revolutionize my field

160

of research and I'm going to get back to do it – by *any means* that's necessary.'

He hesitated, in two minds whether to reveal his great secret.

'You see . . .' he faltered and then looked straight into my tired, aching eyes. 'Everyone else . . . well, Zak Titheridge and Bert Hall, at least – think that the water goes through the cells, but I know that it goes between them and, what is more, can be regulated to suit the physiological needs of the animal. And I can prove it – in the locust rectum – when I get back.'

I reached for the frying pan and Oakley fled, dropping a plastic bag in his haste. I flopped back, utterly exhausted: overwhelmed with the knowledge that I was to be sacrificed for the ultimate truth of the locust rectum.

It was late afternoon when Doris and De Freville returned from their expedition up to the lake. They were very tired, but both in excellent spirits. And they had reason to be, for Doris had knocked over two more whistling ducks.

She set about cooking them as soon as she had reassured herself that I was still alive. Her culinary plans included a broth for me (she prepared it from the livers) and some of the cooked breast which she got De Freville to cut thinly and pound into a sort of pâté. I was able to hold down Doris's concoctions and that, I am convinced, saved my life – but at unthinkable ornithological cost.

We had kept the fire going after our meal and I was sitting up, the first time for several days, enjoying the company and trying not to think of Oakley lurking somewhere in the surrounding darkness waiting to pounce when one or other of us was again brought low. Doris was idly toying with the legs of the whistling duck. They dully reflected the flickering firelight.

Then realization struck. Good God, they were pink – those damned legs were *pink*, like ungainly, garish paddles. According to Hartlaub they should have been bluey-grey and *Dendrocygna arcuata* definitely did not have a white throat patch. Christ, *now* what had we done? There was no other whistling duck like this one, I was sure of it. After all, I had boned up on the Dendrocygnini (to steady my nerves after that business with Muriel Oakley).

Even in my weakened condition, I suspected what I now know to be the case: that those were not the legs of any known species of dendrocygnid – *and Doris had killed them*.

16

I was so appalled by the magnitude of Doris's ornithological crime that I found it difficult to get to sleep that
night, digesting, as I was, what was probably a significant
proportion of the world population of an entirely new
species of bird, which, due to Doris's unerring aim, was
certainly endangered – if not already extinct.

Yet despite awful feelings of guilt I was not above
foolish fantasies of future glory in the pages of the *Ibis* or
Oryx, and fell to naming the duck. Its habits seemed very
different from those of the Wandering Whistling Duck.
In fact, I suspected that it hardly wandered at all or we
would surely have seen it. The Sedentary Whistling Duck
seemed appropriate, but now much better would be *Yeo's*
Whistling Duck (*Dendrocygna yeoi*). What glory to be
remembered with Leach (of forked-tail fame), the blessed
Audubon and his shearwater, or MacGillivary or even
De Freville if it came to that (odd that so many of the
Tubinares should bear human names). At least someone
would have heard of me after I'd gone. Yet, come to
think of it, *I* had not discovered the bird: by rights it
should be Lakowski's Whistling Duck. Yet we could
hardly use Doris's name. After all, she was no ornithologist and had killed three of the birds – but I had eaten
bits from them, so where did that put me? And how was
I going to prove that there ever was such a bird? I could
hardly produce the hacked-off legs or severed heads as
evidence (I would soon become the greatest villain in
modern ornithology) and definitely could not trust De

Freville to keep his mouth shut if I doctored the evidence. I wept a little at the futility of it all and then slipped into uneasy sleep to dream of my childhood on the Wiltshire Downs.

Doris was about early next morning and so was De Freville – Doris saw to that. She had saved a few slices of the breasts from the whistling ducks, and we breakfasted for the first time in two weeks.

I don't know if it was the efforts of the food, for I am not sure whether Doris had told me before of her plan, but I understood for the first time (after breakfast that morning) why she was trying so desperately to cut her way up the mountainside.

'Well, it's just a kinda hunch, really,' she confessed. 'But, you see, if we *are* on Ru-in, like you've said ever since we've been on this stupid island, then we must be about here.'

Doris stabbed her finger at our inadequate map of the archipelago. The island was dumb-bell-shaped and, if Doris was right, then our mountain was somewhere on the grip of the dumb-bell.

'So you see, Doc, if we can hike it over the side of this mountain, then we should be able to see right across to the mainland as well as these islands here.'

De Freville nodded solemnly, clearly impressed by Doris's determination and clarity of purpose.

'If we lit a fire, we could be seen for miles and maybe someone would come and fetch us. If nothin' else, we might find some more of those weird ducks or another of Donald's petrels,' Doris concluded wryly, as she stuffed her sleeping bag into her rucksack and picked up the axe.

'Do you think that you could get up to the lake, Doc?' She tried to sound unconcerned, but I could see that she was still anxious about me. 'It would be safer than leaving

164

you here. If you dozed off the asshole might – well . . .
you know . . .' Doris faltered and then concluded
brightly, 'And if you came up to the lake we wouldn't
have to come back each night *and* you might catch some
fish.'

I felt like a decrepit old-age pensioner faced with
the prospect of a nice Sunday-afternoon stroll up the
Matterhorn. But I got up to the lake. The climb seemed
interminable: over broken slippery rocks and damp gravel
slopes, between clinging creepers and tangled branches
with hideous spikes – tormented by God knows what
insect fiends – and, finally, up what I likened to the north
face of the Eiger, drenched by the drifting spray of the
tumbling waterfall.

I was more dead than alive when I reached Doris's
lake. Yet even in the extremity of my exhaustion I felt the
strange atmosphere of that secret place. It was hemmed in
on three sides by dense greenery which swept from misty
mountain slopes right down to the shore. The water was
still and dark. The only sound was the distant murmur of
the waterfall which poured with glossy smoothness over a
flat stone shelf, some twelve feet wide, overhung with
branches of gnarled trees which clung tenaciously to the
rocky bank. There was no bird song or insect hum, only
occasional gentle ploppings from the obscurity of the
leafy shore.

The lake was long and narrow, perhaps half a mile by
some two hundred yards across at its widest point.
Although still mid-afternoon, the sun had already sunk
behind the peaks to our right, leaving the valley in deep
shadow but still flooding the mist-shrouded summit with
brilliant intensity. The silence was suddenly broken by
the sharp twitter of a Satin Flycatcher close at hand in
the undergrowth. I remember thinking what a ridiculously

165

appropriate setting it was for this enigmatic bird. I balked at the thought of consuming such a precious morsel, if Doris's aim should prove equal to bringing down the elusive creature (originally named after Victoria, Crown Princess of Germany, and variously classified with the Saxicolinae, the birds of paradise, warblers or even chat-thrushes). But Doris was busy laying out our gear on a low ferny outcrop close to the waterfall.

There was not much to lay out, for we had taken only basic essentials, in Doris's and De Freville's rucksacks: sleeping bags, first-aid kit, the saucepan, one torch, matches, De Freville's binoculars, the axe, our mess tins, knife, fishing tackle – and the mugs, of course. Doris had prudently saved some scraps of gristle and burnt skin from the whistling ducks to use for my fishing. De Freville baited the hook for me and tossed the line into the dark water at the only place where we could crawl to the shore, beneath low spreading branches, some hundred yards from the waterfall.

They left me there, perched uncomfortably on a mossy mound at the water's edge while they went to explore. It was difficult even to sit up, so low were the branches pressing down, and eventually I lay full length along the mound, which was just about the length of a man. The float remained vertical and motionless, a slim red and white pencil exactly mirrored in the dark water. I was desperately tired but did not doze as I was so prone to do before. Food had evidently changed all that. Worse, I felt hunger pangs returning with the familiar abdominal cramps spreading up to my shoulders. I had been spared these pains for some time, but now that I had broken my enforced fast they returned, and with them came a desolate conviction of the utter hopelessness of our position.

I suppose that I had been buoyed up by Doris's optimistic plan, but as I sprawled on the mound at the water's edge, I saw the foolishness of her scheme and knew that we were lost. She always had been impetuously wrong-headed in supervisions (as in that stupid argument with De Freville about Bess of Hardwick). Now she had led us up into this secret place where we would be beyond all finding and where even our mouldering remains would never be seen by human eyes.

It was at that exact moment that I saw the leg bone sticking out from another mound, half-covered with ferns and tangled creepers, and then, a second later, the empty eye sockets of a human skull, brown and discoloured, at the crumbling edge of yet another mound further along the bank, half-veiled by a close green canopy.

In my fright, I reared up, banging my head against a branch and scratching my face with countless prickly leaves. Two tiny lizards fell, like floppy fairground novelties, on to my neck. I screeched with terror but stood trapped as in a dreadful nightmare of an iron maiden of thorny spikes and crawling reptiles.

'Doris,' I croaked. 'Doris – get me out of here.'

'That you, Doc?' Her shout was close at hand, only yards away it seemed.

'*Of course* it's me, you silly bitch. Get me out of this.'

'There's no need to carry on like that. What's the matter?'

Her voice, bossy and schoolmarmish, brought me to my senses and I sat down abruptly, scratching my face and ears in the process.

'It's all right,' I gasped. 'I sort of banged my head.'

I heard a crashing of branches and then De Freville's face appeared. He was kneeling down peering anxiously at me.

'You've scratched yourself,' he announced accusingly.

'You shouldn't do that,' Doris's voice came from behind, 'these thorns might be poisonous for all you know.'

'All right, all right,' I groaned.

'Anyway,' De Freville commenced, as he used to when making a telling historical point in supervision classes. '*Anyway*, it seems that we are in some sort of ancient burial place. I'm surprised that I didn't notice it yesterday. There are mounds and bones everywhere – *hundreds* of them. I shouldn't be surprised if this is not a major archaeological find.'

We had lizards for supper that night. They were everywhere: tiny little fellows, only three inches long, with dark stripes on their greenish bodies and bright yellow eyes. So tame were they that we could get to within a foot of them, but they would dart off when we came closer or made a grab for them. Doris got them in the end, by an impressive display of marksmanship involving a stealthy approach and a quick whack between the eyes with a pebble from the catapult. She killed dozens of the creatures by dusk and stewed them in lake water on a smoking fire that took De Freville some time to start, so damp was the wood in that place.

I am amazed that I could scrunch through such a frightful meal and still feel distinctly queasy to recall it. But I had already tasted flesh after so many days of starvation and the lust for food was on me. I would have had no compunction in eating another whistling duck, if there had been any.

It came on to drizzle in the evening as the rain clouds lowered from the mountain slopes. I lay in the darkness in my wet sleeping bag (inwardly cursing De Freville as

168

he rabbited on about those blasted graves and scattered bones) in a nightmare of superstitious dread and severe indigestion. I knew that we were engaged in a most desperate gamble for survival. My face was a torment of scratches. I imagined the ghosts of the dead rising up in the surrounding darkness, while De Freville droned on about the likelihood of the graves being those of pre-Melanesian peoples.

That night I dreamed that the risen inhabitants of the graves were all armed with plastic bags and woke frequently to peer into the drizzling blackness while Doris snored at my side.

The following morning, I insisted on accompanying Doris on her foray to the other end of the lake. The rain had cleared in the night and the waxy leaves were jewelled with countless sparkling raindrops as the sunlight penetrated the morning shadows of our hidden valley. Doris was very put out at the prospect of my assistance, but, I maintained, I had been much recovered by the whistling ducks and lizard stew and that it would do me good to get some exercise. I was definitely *not* going to stay by myself in that fearful boneyard. So it was that De Freville remained behind to fish and to whack away at the lizards with Doris's catapult, while she and I crawled and cut our way out, yard by painful yard, through tangled vegetation.

I had to rest frequently and, I must admit, contributed little to the tunnel through the trees. Yet I kept at it and was back at work the next day as well, after another lizard supper and a soggy night of superstitious dreads. In fact, it was on the second day that I made a major contribution to our efforts. It must have been about midday, for the sun was shining directly into the valley, which was as hot as a steam bath. My job was to clear away the branches and brushwood that Doris chopped free. I was pushing it into the vegetation at either side of the green tunnel which we were making, first to the left and then to the right. It was while I was pushing a largish branch to the right that I glimpsed, from our gloomy corridor, an expanse of pebbles and small rocks, lit by a shaft of brilliant sunlight.

I shoved my way through a pliant screen of large waxy leaves and found myself standing in the open in blinding sunshine. It was like an escape from a tomb. Pebbles and scattered boulders stretched away for several hundred yards, scoured out, I guessed, by intermittent floods from the high mountains. To my utter relief (for I was despairing) I realized that this strange causeway ran, more or less, in the direction in which we had been heading: as far as I could judge, right to the foot of the steep slope, the top of which was our objective.

It took only a few minutes, instead of uncomfortable days of slavery in the tunnel, to reach the wall of greenery that barred our way on the last stage of Doris's reckless venture.

We did not attempt to battle up the mountainside in the afternoon heat, for even Doris had been tired by our exertions. I was so fatigued that I could hardly walk back to the camp. There we found De Freville sitting happily amongst those macabre tombs, with one end of the fishing line tied to his foot, while he thwacked away with Doris's catapult at the lizards. He had certainly been restored by the diet of whistling ducks, his family petrel and innumerable lizards.

De Freville was delighted with the news of our latest discovery which, he gloated, would now hasten us to our objective. But it was not going to be that easy. I could see that the upward scramble for several hundred feet through dense vegetation at an angle of 60° was going to be the worst of our labours. Furthermore, I was far from convinced that it would lead anywhere. Even if it did, we could not be sure that we would have the fine view of the mainland or the other islands which Doris imagined. There could well be another ridge behind this one. Furthermore, if it was as Doris believed, then it was unlikely that the smoke of our fire would be visible so many miles away – assuming that there was someone there to see it. All that we had done was to waste our energies, yet again, and make it virtually impossible for anyone to find us in that terrible tangled wilderness.

We started out again soon after dawn the next morning. There was a thick mist from which the gnarled trees loomed like misshapen claws festooned and interspersed with countless bizarre shapes. De Freville came along as well, carefully carrying a saucepan of stewed lizards for our evening meal. Doris said that we could drink the liquor, cold, for soup and then chew away at the tiny soggy corpses – a sort of dreadful reptilian whitebait. I remember thinking that in College they would just be sitting down for dinner at the High Table and imagined Cecil Fox toying with his chilled melon and pestering some of the young Fellows to play bowls with him afterwards. There would be the familiar clicking sounds and the scent of summer flowers as the shadows lengthened on the smooth grass in the Fellows' garden.

Very sensibly, De Freville persuaded Doris not to rush headlong into the thicket, after we had stumbled along the uneven causeway in grey swirling mist. De Freville argued that there must be dried-out water courses hidden in the dense vegetation which had fed the torrents that had scoured out the bare causeway. And he was right, for within twenty minutes we discovered a narrow boulder-strewn gully which led upwards under a canopy of over-hanging branches. We crawled on all fours for at least a couple of hundred feet before we were once again faced with seemingly impenetrable undergrowth. This time it was a matter of hacking our way upwards and pulling away the broken branches, tenacious vines and stinging creepers that left my hands a mass of scarlet weals.

We stopped as the mist lifted, towards the end of the afternoon. It was back-breaking work and poor Doris was pretty well played out. I suppose we must have advanced about fifty yards from where the vegetation closed in on us.

Supper that night was not as awful as I had feared. The lizard soup was quite palatable, not unlike turtle consommé, and I was getting used to crushing tiny reptile bones. It wasn't so much the breaking of them in the mouth, it was the swallowing that was so difficult. I was worried that one of the bones might get stuck in my throat or give me appendicitis so I chewed thoroughly before swallowing and suffered no ill effects.

We slept at the entrance to the gully, under a low covering of leaves that gave us some protection against the rain which fell quite heavily during the night. The morning was clear and the sun soon drove the mist completely from the summit, above us and to our right. Nothing else was good that morning. My hands were swollen to twice their normal size and one of the spots on De Freville's right ankle had swollen and was oozing. We had no food and no water, for we could not find a way to the shore of the lake from where we were. Worse than everything I was utterly convinced of the futility of our efforts. Why had we been so stupid as to move from our camp near the sea shore? If a search party arrived they would find no trace of us – just the empty tents – and it was a damned sight more pleasant place to die than this ghastly hole.

We sucked rain drops from the leaves. They tasted bitter and were probably poisonous, but I was beyond all caring. Doris and De Freville were determined to carry on.

'Hell, Doc,' she said. 'We can't be far from the top now. We're aiming at the lowest point on this ridge. Just one more push . . . and . . . then we shall know . . .'

Her faltering confirmed my fears. She was no more convinced than I was about this whole dreadful business. It was just her foolhardy impetuosity. I had seen it very clearly in the very first essays that she had written for me in College and yet I had allowed myself to be led by the nose to this. Muriel had said that the Lakowski girl was dangerous and she had been damned well right.

However, I was certain about one thing – I was not going back by myself to that spooky graveyard.

So I stayed on with De Freville and Doris, in the last phase of their reckless venture. I was so dispirited that I made no real efforts to help in their bush-whacking. Occasionally, I would shift a branch or pull away at a creeper, but my swollen hands were so painful that even this was purgatory. For most of the time I just squatted on my haunches inwardly bemoaning my fate and the certainty of a lingering death in the undergrowth.

It was while I was so engaged that I spotted the first of the snakes. It was wriggling on the ground behind me and there were two more behind it. They were brown, indeterminate and not more than two feet long, but they were snakes and that was enough for me. I dived headlong into the undergrowth to my left and sat down, quivering, on a wide stone step.

My companions were, apparently, amazed by my abrupt disappearance. Doris said afterwards that they heard my shout, but when they looked back there was no sign of me.

'*Now* where in the hell have you gone, Doc?' Doris bawled. It sounded rather ill-natured, I thought, as I sat in the green gloom looking anxiously round for more snakes.

'Just resting,' I managed to shout back. 'And keeping away from those damned snakes.'

'Hell,' I heard her mutter. 'He really is nuts.'

She raised her voice.

'*There are no snakes here*, Doc. And what are you doing in there, anyway? Jesus!'

'Yes, well I'll be out in a minute,' I called back, trying desperately to sound matter-of-fact.

I had always been terrified of snakes, even of grass-snakes as a boy in North Wiltshire, and I was not going to take a chance now. I looked round anxiously to make sure that none was sliding down the steps towards me.

Then it dawned on me. Steps! *I was sitting on a long stone stairway*, going straight up the slope towards what looked like clear daylight.

'I've found a row of steps,' I called out. 'In here – about the same width as O Staircase in College.'

'Jesus,' I heard Doris say. 'Go and see what he's up to, will you, Donald?'

De Freville's long camel face pushed through the leafy curtain. He looked cross, like a tired child who was made to do the washing-up. Then his eyes grew round with wonder.

'He's right. He's sitting on a row of bloody steps . . . about the same size as O Staircase . . . sorry, Doc . . .'

De Freville pitched forward, nearly landing in my lap, as Doris pushed her way in.

'My God!' was the only comment that she could muster in the face of the undoubted reality of my seat.

17

De Freville had been enthusiastic about the graveyard; he was ecstatic about the stone stairway. He worked out that the gully must have run across the slope and that we had followed its direction to encounter the steps. According to him, they must run straight up the mountain slope, exactly from the end of the lake. So (reasoned De Freville), the graveyard, the stairs and the lake itself represented one huge monument. The flat stone shelf over which the waterfall flowed, at the other end of the lake, was undoubtedly also of some great significance, he maintained.

I held my head in my hands, still squatting on my stone step, while De Freville raved on as I remembered him doing about the origins of Lollardy.

So many thoughts crowded into my mind. Somehow, it seemed, there was a mysterious symbolism for me in this place which was related to all that had happened before and since we had been on the island. First, there was Cecil Fox, whose enmity (especially about that crucial meeting of the carpet committee) had got me on to the island, as it had Doris and De Freville – according to what Muriel Oakley had told me when she had last appeared. Then there was that mix-up with Muriel and the killing of the Mara, so swiftly followed by the tidal wave and, then, Oakley's treachery. All these things had driven us remorselessly to this place, first to the grotto where even Doris had felt an unseen presence (*and I had seen it*) and then up by the waterfall to that terrible lake and the graveyard, then the hidden causeway, now to these damned steps going to goodness knows what.

Doris's reactions were quite different.

'Are you two going to move your *asses*?'

I shifted uncomfortably, grey and middle-aged, fearful of what was going to happen to us.

'*And* you, Donald.'

De Freville rose to a half-crouch, his eyes still shining.

Doris turned, to become our leader, wielding the axe against the branches and vines that barred our way to where I could see the clear light of day above our heads.

It took only a few minutes for Doris to cut her way up those last few ancient steps. De Freville and I came behind the small vigorous figure with her dark hair flying, once again witch-like, as she had been when she joined in the killing of the Mara. Slowly, De Freville and I followed, step by step – to what I could not imagine.

Doris severed the final obstructing branch with a single blow of the axe and stepped forward on what seemed to be a large stone platform, some twenty feet across and as many deep. High cliffs of bare red rock rose above us to left and right.

'Come on, you guys – this is it,' Doris whispered.

I could feel that she too was overawed. The air was clean and fresh and smelt of sea.

We walked, side by side, across the rocky platform towards the far edge and then, simultaneously, looked down.

There, hundreds of feet below, was a golf course – as green and neat as you could wish. It was smooth and undulating, dotted with groups of palm trees. Here and there were regular oval patches of light-coloured sand, and mechanical trolleys moving slowly across the greens like children's toys. There were people, one in scarlet,

177

another all in yellow, moving against the unnatural greenness.

'Christ,' said De Freville.

It was all that could be said: we were all too absorbed by what lay before us.

I could see several groups of buildings away towards the sea shore which curved round to form a wide bay from the western end of the island. De Freville handed me his binoculars. I focused painfully with swollen lacerated fingers. There were rows of tiny thatched umbrellas sticking out at one end of a long sandy beach with people in bathing costumes sitting under them and waiters in grass skirts moving about with trays of glasses held above their heads. I saw shady palm groves and the turquoise glimpse of a swimming pool. Scattered white triangles moved slowly across the bay, with tiny figures clinging to them. A neat gravel road snaked its way between closely trimmed grass, dotted with frangipani and hibiscus trees. There were low clipped hedges and circular flowerbeds; blue striped awnings shading long flagged terraces; ponies cantering along the shore; there were white painted chalets tastefully grouped under huge protective palms and lawn sprinklers and a green-aproned gardener with a laden wheel-barrow.

I shall remember that scene until my dying day. Even so I still find it hard to believe in its reality. There was certainly no sign of it on our ten-year-old map of the archipelago. And why had no one appeared on our side of the island? I should have remembered the article in the February issue of *Country Life*; the one about how 'tourism in Manabau was deliberately confined to a single island – the greater part of which was a national nature reserve'. But I did not, because I was tired, confused and still very frightened – as Doris certainly was not. She was

178

'madder than hell', for although the paradoxical scene below us had more than vindicated her reckless plan there was still the problem of how to get to it, down several hundred feet or so of sheer cliff.

'A goddam fly couldn't crawl down there,' Doris bawled, recoiling from the vertiginous edge. 'But I'm not going to leave until someone down there sees us. So let's get on with the bonfire, like we planned in the first place.'

De Freville got the fire going with surprising ease. There were enough dry twigs and leaves littered around to start a blaze which soon yielded a spectacular plume of smoke when we tossed on branch after branch of greenery, frantically wrenched and chopped from the nearby trees. The smoke billowed splendidly into the clear air and then drifted lazily among the trees as we waved and choked on the rocky platform.

'We're not going to leave until we're seen,' Doris repeated belligerently. 'Get your binoculars on the goings-on down there, Donald, and let us know when they've spotted us.'

Small groups of miniature golfers were coming and going all the time as we waved and danced, hundreds of feet above their heads, beneath our gigantic smoke signal.

For an hour or more we plied our bonfire with fresh branches and green leaves while poor De Freville kept his eyes glued on the immediate golfing scene.

'Always thought that it was a bloody stupid sport,' he grumbled, shifting uncomfortably on the platform's edge.

'It's a goddam *marvellous* sport if it gets us out of this mess,' Doris retorted, signalling irritably for poor De Freville to turn his binoculars on a largish group, of a dozen or so, which had appeared on one of the nearer greens.

'Well, that's about all you can say for it,' De Freville replied, turning to glare at Doris.

'Will you please keep your beady little eyes on that lot down there – you jerk,' Doris roared.

'They're doing something, aren't they?' I said.

'Yes, you're right, Dr Yeo. They're waving. Well at least some of them are and they seem to be looking upwards. One of them certainly *is* and he is swinging his stick . . . club . . . over his head.'

'Go on, Donald, what are they doing now?'

'They're all waving – all of them.'

'Now, Doc, start pointing.'

Doris was jumping up and down in her excitement: the second time that I had witnessed this.

'Pointing? What at?'

'Pointing *there* – that way – *over there* of course.'

Doris was waving her hand back in the direction of the interior of the island. I joined in.

'Why are we doing this, Doris?'

'Doc, you really are a yo-yo. We are pointing to show where we have come from (obviously) and where we are going (*obviously*) and in which direction they will be able to find us, because we can't get down there by jumping off this lousy cliff – OBVIOUSLY.'

'All right, Doris, all right. There was no need for that.' I hastily resumed pointing as Doris intended.

'What are they doing now, Donald?'

'They're all walking back to that thatched bungalow. Two of them are running. Oh, now the rest are running too.'

'Great, great,' Doris exulted, executing a theatrical bow to the world in general. 'Let's get over the other side to meet the rescue party. Now move your *ass*, Donald De Freville.' So it was that we all moved ourselves (as

Doris had so coarsely suggested to De Freville) back down the stone steps, then along the gully on to the causeway and through the leafy tunnel to the top of the waterfall, which we reached at dusk.

There was no possibility of food that evening, but we drank mug after mug of cool lake water before slipping into our sleeping bags for another dismal night of drizzle.

The next morning, which was clear and sunny, we continued our descent, scrambling and slithering down the steep rocky slope to our tents by the grotto. We washed ourselves free of dust, smuts and mud in the waterfall and set about rebuilding the signal fire and, also, sticking a long line of mangrove poles across the beach, two with ragged shirts tied on for makeshift flags. I cannot imagine why we had not done this before.

There was no sign of Oakley or any indication that he had been to our camp. All was as we had left it, with our few useless possessions neatly stacked within the hot tents.

We were desperately tired after our exertions in the mountains. My mutilated face, neck and hands were still extremely painful despite much dabbing by Doris with the antiseptic from the first-aid kit. Yet we kept going, occasionally walking along the beach and climbing across the still formidable wreckage of the tidal wave to get an earlier view of, and to signal to, the rescue craft.

All that long afternoon we waited, our excitement mounting. De Freville was already planning his first meal of steak, egg and chips, followed by pineapple and lager on the hotel terrace which he had spotted through the binoculars; Doris was dreaming of the swimming pool with a plate of hamburgers and a six-pack of Cola-Cola, al fresco. I dared not hope for anything, for my doubts were returning. Particularly, the dismal realization that smoke from however large a bonfire probably looks remarkably like clinging mountain mists when it filters through the surrounding vegetation and that golfers might well wave their clubs for reasons quite unconnected with the appearance of three insignificant midgets on a mountainside hundreds of feet above their heads. Under the circumstances I would willingly have traded my companions' gastronomic fantasies for the reality of a nice plate of lizard stew. But then I am a realist and always knew that something nasty would get me in the end.

For two interminable days we waited for the rescuers.

At first my companions kept up their foolish hopes. The golfers had seen our signals, De Freville was sure of that; it was a large island, it would take time to find us. There had been no suitable boat to sail round this far, they would have to radio Manau, Doris maintained with growing uncertainty. Then De Freville tried another tack. There was no sign of Oakley: he had not lurked around, as before, had obviously not been to the camp in our absence and we had found no footprints on the beach – or his body. *Ergo*, Oakley had been taken off while we were away and might even now be in Manau, from which a craft would be swiftly dispatched as soon as it was known that a De Freville was cast away on Ru-in.

And so they rambled on, as we waited, our hunger growing, in the frighteningly damp heat. By the second evening I was more convinced than ever that our position was hopeless. Eventually Doris succumbed to a bout of savage tears and then decided that she and De Freville would climb back to the lake to catch lizards. Strangely, no one could face the prospect of another tantalizing view from the rocky platform on the mountain.

They left me early on the third morning, once more

lying limply on my sleeping bag. I was now nearly as weak as I had been before, when I believed that I was near the end. It was not only the return to starvation which had brought me low, it was sharing the bitter disappointment of my young companions and, I suppose, the snuffing out of the tiny glimmer of hope which also lay beneath my black conviction of doom.

Doris had made me promise that although I could relax, I would keep a sharp look-out when they were away lizarding. I was supposed to walk down to the beach with my sleeping bag and continue my rest there, but with my eyes open at all times.

I did not go down immediately. The day had not long broken and I wanted to think and to sleep a little before hobbling to the top of the beach. There was so much to straighten out in my mind, for I did not want to expire like an animal brought unknowing to its end. I thought of Molly and wondered if she was anxious at receiving only that one postcard from me so many weeks ago: I should have left some with Rua to post every week. Poor Molly, how she would have loved a holiday at that place on the other side of the island. But she would never have got me into somewhere like that: for evening drinks at the Beachcomber Bar with fat golfing solicitors from Iowa and their raddled blue-rinsed wives in Bermuda shorts who would make insincere promises 'to keep in touch after the vacation'. Yet, what right had a broken-down academic to be so damned superior? I suppose it was just sour grapes because we could never afford to go to places like that, or almost any other place if it came to that. How ironic if they buried my whitened bones on the edge of the fifteenth green. Cecil Fox would see the funny side of that. According to what Rua had said, they finished off sinners on Ru-in. So, even my little misunderstanding with Muriel Oakley might be settled here. Perhaps that is what all those graves were doing up by that awful lake: the remains of hundreds of poor devils, trapped into nasty ends by their frail human desires. It was a lousy arrangement.

I drifted into a familiar starvation doze, again conscious of the closeness of an unseen presence. It could not be Muriel Oakley; it felt quite different, and, in any case, her final appearance had been definitely scheduled for the 'thirteenth day', which was long passed.

The sun was shining straight on to my face when I awoke again, from a dream of Cecil Fox as Prospero controlling all the terrible events of the past weeks. I put my face in my hands and once more drifted into troubled sleep, wishing never to awake.

18

I woke again, this time to the shaking of my right shoulder and the sound of a woman's voice.

'Are you all right?'

It was an English voice: soft, with clipped tones, but definite and bossy.

I jerked my shoulder away from the hand.

'God, you gave me a turn, just lying there like that.'

I stayed motionless, my face still buried in my poor swollen hands.

'Who are you?' I said, fearful of what had now come to me.

'I'm Miranda – second in command around here . . .'

I groaned and twisted on my filthy sleeping bag to see a pair of startlingly blue eyes staring at me from a plump freckled face.

'You *can't* be,' I groaned. 'Did Cecil Fox send you?'

'Fox? *Cecil* Fox? Never heard of him. He's certainly not in the Service.'

She helped me into a sitting position. I noticed that she was blonde, her hair tucked neatly under a floppy bush hat which shaded a broad, rather squashed-up nose.

'Well, as I said, I'm Miranda – Miranda Ogilvy, actually – of the National Park Service. What on earth are you doing here?'

'We're on an expedition. We got shipwrecked.'

'*We?* Are there more of you? You know that you shouldn't be here . . . you're going to be in *fearful* trouble, I'm afraid.'

Even in my weakness, I saw outrage in her eyes and in the hard set of her mouth. There was going to be trouble all right. Her face softened while she fished about in a canvas shoulder bag.

'Here, have some Kendal mint cake. I always carry some, It's one of my few vices.'

She popped a piece into my mouth: a familiar minty comfort spread through my tired body.

'Now, who are you?'

'Yeo, James Yeo. There are two others. My students – Doris Lakowski and Donald De Freville . . .' I looked round in the direction of the waterfall.

'They're not up there, are they?'

I nodded weakly.

'Hell!'

'Hell? Why hell?'

'Because no one goes up there, *no one*. And that's all I know really, except that it was where the Chiefs were buried in the olden times and where they killed the Reverend Mr Skinner in 1885. It's out of bounds – even for the Park Service – and that's that as far as I'm concerned.'

She paused and popped another lump of mint cake into my ulcerated mouth.

'It's all a lot of nonsense. But – thank goodness – my boatman isn't an islander, so he won't make any trouble. He's Indian, actually. There are lots of them here.'

She seemed quite unconcerned with my weakened condition and prattled on about how we should have got permission from the National Park Service to sail around the archipelago and how it was 'typical' that the 'people' at the Institute had not thought to tell 'them' about our expedition. There was, I gathered, no love lost between the two organizations. According to Miranda, this was

186

entirely due to the megalomania of the Samoan Director of MITME. She seemed very pleased when she learned that we had wrecked the Institute boat.

Miranda was astonished by the devastation left by the tidal wave. 'They' had not known about it at National Park HQ. It must have been a very local affair, she said.

It appeared that Miranda had been away, on leave in England (she came from Worcestershire), or else she would have come earlier on one of her regular tours of inspection of the islands. There were more than two hundred of them, she said, and there was only one really sea-worthy craft 'in the Service'. It also seemed that Miranda's Manabauan colleagues were not particularly keen to leave their desks, or the flesh pots of Manau, hence my rescuer was a very busy young woman.

Eventually, she got fed up with waiting and started to carry my gear down to the shore. I took the opportunity to fling the legs of Yeo's Whistling Duck and the battered head of De Freville's Petrel into the undergrowth.

Miranda helped me down to where a spotless white dinghy was dragged up on the beach. A long grey launch was moored beyond the reef. A tall Indian in khaki shorts and a dazzling orange T-shirt was sitting, idly smoking, on the stern of the dinghy. He had already stowed my grubby equipment. When he saw us creeping slowly across the hot sand he pushed the craft into the waves and then returned to carry me, like a child, to the boat, dumping me uncomfortably against the bow. We shot across the lagoon, the outboard absolutely flat out, the spray stinging my ears. To my relief we slowed and merely whizzed through the break in the reef that we had negotiated with such great care and high hopes in the old *Bounty II* so many weeks before.

Rampal (he had told me his name) made me several

cups of sweet Indian tea and heated two tins of tomato soup on the stove in the launch's tiny galley. I finished off the meal with some oatmeal biscuits and then lay down on a bunk in the main cabin, watching the reflected sunlight flicker on the ceiling and enjoying the gentle rocking of the boat. Everything was so neat and clean. You couldn't even smell the sea. I noticed that Miranda had pinned up a photograph of Worcester Cathedral and that Hartlaub's book lay open on the table. I shuddered to think what might have happened if I had not disposed of those legs and the head before coming aboard. I hoped to God that Doris and De Freville would keep their mouths shut when they reappeared.

It seemed odd, lying there entirely confined by man-made things without the smells and sounds that had been with me for so many days: the continual hubbub of falling water, the evening breeze rustling the ferns above our heads in the grotto, the distant call of wading birds and the smell of rain on red dusty soil.

Incredibly, I was almost nostalgic for what had been a hellish nightmare.

My thoughts were abruptly terminated by a bumping against the hull and raised voices.

'They're *my* lizards, I tell you. Leave them alone or you'll regret it.'

Doris was in full voice – and so evidently was Miranda Ogilvy.

'You're *not* taking reptiles from a National Park Reserve and that's that.'

'They're dead, aren't they? So what the hell?'

'Look, you're in enough trouble already – what with illegally entering, *and camping in*, a National Park Nature Reserve – and you'll be in a devil of a lot more if you take out those lizards.'

188

'Go to hell!'

'What were you going to do with them anyway?'

'*Eat* them of course.'

'No, you're not. How disgusting.'

'Who's going to stop me I'd like to know . . .'

And so it went on; it seemed, for some minutes.

Eventually, Miranda got the upper hand, but not without naked bribery in the form of two cans of Coca-Cola and a tin of Bourbon biscuits (which Miranda said she had bought in Tewkesbury the previous week).

It was a shook to see Doris and De Freville sitting so awkwardly on the dark-blue upholstered seat each clutching a Coca-Cola can and stuffing Bourbon biscuits. They looked terrible. De Freville's beard was black and shapeless, like an obscene fungus, his uncut fingernails curved like filthy talons. Doris's thin face was streaked with grime, her long hair matted. I could tell that she was still furious at the loss of her precious reptiles and leaned over to touch her hand: I knew how much those lizards meant to her. She looked up, a grin slowly spreading across her grubby face.'

'Well, we made it, Doc.'

De Freville seemed to be trying to impress Miranda Ogilvy.

'. . . yes, I suppose you could regard it as our totem bird. Actually, I've always wanted to find the family petrel . . .'

I managed to kick De Freville, beneath the table. Fortunately his surprised yelp was lost in the excitement caused by the entry of Rampal with tea and more bowls of tomato soup.

While the others were slurping their soup, Miranda told what was to happen to us. Our crime was very great, apparently. There would be a stiff fine and, if we could

189

not pay: gaol. So, although it clearly went against the grain, our rescuer was going to make things easier for us.

'I'm not going to take you back to Manau, because I would have to report all that has happened and it would also mean that I would lose a lot of time in the field. The bureaucracy is pretty formidable here, I can tell you.'

We nodded gratefully. De Freville was particularly affected by Miranda's unexpected leniency.

'Secondly, I shall go back to the other bay and put you off at the Coral Strand.'

'Oh God, not marooning us again,' Doris wailed.

'No, silly. The Coral Strand is the biggest and swankiest hotel over there. They will look after you. Go to the Director of Tourism – his office is there. He will get you off when the hydrofoil comes over from the mainland.'

Miranda sipped her tea thoughtfully. I suspected that she was surprised by her uncharacteristic generosity; it must have broken practically every section of the *National Park Code*, which I had just noticed pinned to a bulkhead.

'You can *say*', Miranda said, her face puckering at the outrageous illegality of it all, 'that I picked you up on the other side of the creek at the west end of this bay. It's the only part of the Reserve in which tourists are allowed: with a guide – *of course*.'

'Come to think of it,' Miranda continued, 'why on earth didn't you wade across the creek, instead of sitting up where I found you? You could have easily got round to the tourist section from there.'

'Because of the crocodiles,' I blurted out. 'Then we got sort of confused what with starving and everything – and there were no hotels marked on our map . . .'

'Crocodiles. Did you say crocodiles?'

'Yes, marine crocodiles,' De Freville joined in. 'We heard one in the creek – a sort of coughing noise.'

Miranda sniggered.

'Look, take my word for it, there are *no* crocodiles within a thousand miles of here.'

'Well, it sounded like one,' De Freville persisted. 'A sort of coughing noise . . .'

It had been Oakley, the zoologist, who had convinced us that there were crocodiles in that damned creek. *Crocodylus porosus*, he had said: they could swim enormous distances.

I realized that we had not mentioned Oakley's existence – and had no intention of doing so. Things were complicated enough as they were. After all, he had left *us* to perish and now he could have a dose of his own medicine, at least until we saw fit to get him off – that is, if he was still on the island. In any case, I was in no mood to meet the man. Maybe I would feel more generous after civilized food, rest and a good bath, but certainly not now.

Rampal brought the boat carefully up to the hydrofoil jetty, the nearest mooring to the Coral Strand. From the deck I could see great wonders; some of which I had spotted from the mountain and had then despaired of ever seeing again. There was the jetty itself, for example, a miraculous construction of smooth concrete, paving stones and carefully shaped coral, with white-painted railings and stone steps.

As Rampal held on to the rope, which he had passed through a mooring ring, Miranda gave us one last piece of advice, or perhaps more accurately, an ultimatum.

'I'm not coming ashore. This way I don't have to tell any untruths. But it's done on one condition, that you *never* tell anyone that you were in the Reserve *or* that you ever went on to the mountain from where I found you. OK?'

'OK,' we chorused and waved as Rampal cast off and headed the long grey launch towards the open sea.

'Stupid bitch,' Doris growled. The loss of those lizards evidently still rankled.

19

We left our gear on the jetty, where Rampal had dumped it, and walked slowly towards the hotel. The path, or I suppose more accurately the drive, curved between tall palms towards low, wide steps set exactly in the middle of a long wooden veranda. We trod on a dark mixture of leaf mould and wood shavings, deliciously soft underfoot. On each side were smooth lawns dotted with scattered beds of scarlet flowers and large shrubs with huge waxy leaves and small white flowers. The murmur of the surf was distant and subdued. Advancing towards us was a tall figure, almost Roman in its dignity, dark of skin with black bushy hair that stood far out from the head. He wore stout black sandals with enormous brass buckles. His dark-green skirt was edged with a regular geometric pattern of gold. The shiny buttons on his short scarlet jacket gleamed in the afternoon sunlight.

'Are you guests at the Coral Strand?'

'No,' I said. 'We are shipwrecked mariners and we are looking for the Director of Tourism.'

'Was he expecting you, sir?' There was a just perceptible pause before the 'sir'.

'No, you see, it's difficult – by the very nature of the event – to make appointments when you're shipwrecked. And we are very tired.'

He gave me a pained smile. I sensed that I might have to pay for my flippancy.

'I will enquire whether Mr Truscott will see you. Would you please be so kind as to follow me?'

We followed him through a vast lobby. Its sloping roof was supported by what appeared to be piled wooden pineapples, one on top of the other from floor to ceiling, marvellous in their detail, curved from single tree trunks. The reception desk was a war canoe floating on potted ferns, its bottom cut away to allow for frizzy-haired receptionists to stand to their duties, with telephones at hand in the elaborately carved bow and stern. One corner of the lobby was a jungle; another the fo'c'sle of a brigantine; a third the Somerset Maugham Bar.

We were taken behind a screen of festooned fishing nets to a white sliding door, such as might be found in a warehouse. It opened into a long bare corridor lit only from above by glass fanlights. Our guide stopped at the second door on the right, indicating that we should wait. He tapped and paused respectfully at an unpainted wooden door. A man's deep voice told him to enter and he did so.

There followed a rather complex sequence of comings-and-goings. First, our guide emerged and then disappeared through the sliding door back into the lobby. Next, the unpainted door opened and a sallow woman's face, quizzical and bespectacled, stared at us from a half-opened door before she quietly closed it, leaving us again alone in the silence of the bleak corridor. Then the sliding door moved again to reveal a small, heavy-jowled man, totally bald and wearing gold-rimmed spectacles, followed by the skirted guide, by whom he had evidently been sought. They were both admitted to the room with the unpainted door which, I supposed, in the fullness of time, we would also enter.

De Freville had by this time slumped to a sitting position on the floor; Doris was pacing up and down like a caged animal.

'What the hell is going on around here? I'm *starving* and I need the can – I've been looking forward to *that* for weeks.'

She collided with the magnificent man in the skirt as he emerged (rather abruptly, I thought) into the corridor and disappeared as swiftly into the gloom behind the fishing net tableau, closing the sliding door with a thud.

For a full ten minutes more we waited in that damned corridor. I felt filthy and dreadful in every imaginable way. My legs ached; my head was throbbing. More than anything, I desired coffee: cupfuls of the stuff, freshly-ground and black, scalding hot and extravagantly sweet. I was faint for want of it.

No coffee materialized. Instead, the unpainted door opened again. The bald man had evidently said all that he had to say to the deep-voiced man and, for all we knew, to the bespectacled woman. He too disappeared through the sliding door.

Yet still we were not admitted to the forbidden room.

The sunlight was already tinting the bare walls with evening colours before the final moves were made that would decide our fate.

The first was the appearance of a fresh participant: an impressively tall Manabauan, in a khaki uniform with the words 'Security Guard' emblazoned in dark-blue letters on his shoulder. He was immediately shown into the room that we could not enter. Our original guide (who had brought him) remained, standing outside the unpainted door glaring at us, I thought, in an insolent and distinctly hostile manner.

After five more anxious minutes, the security man came out into the corridor. Behind him stood the owner of the incredibly deep voice, Truscott himself.

Truscott was as tall as his companion, but much more

heavily built. He was a fleshy man, with a florid complexion, sparse sandy hair and, above all ludicrous things, a monocle. I hated him on sight. Unfortunately, the feeling seemed to be reciprocal.

'And *you*, I presume, are Dr Yeo. With, no doubt, your two students.'

He cleared his throat, moved closer to me and boomed away at point-blank range, smelling of garlic and whisky.

'I must say that I never thought you'd have the nerve to turn up here. It's the very last thing I would have expected from what Dr Oakley has told me.'

None of us spoke. Even Doris was momentarily lost for words.

'Not surprisingly, Dr Oakley does not wish to see you . . .'

'That's big of him – real big,' Doris spluttered.

'And we certainly don't want to see him,' said De Freville.

This enraged Truscott.

'Wipe that silly smile off your face, young man,' he blared, quite oblivious of the conflicting emotions that were in reality flitting over De Freville's grimy face. Outrage, confusion and despair were certainly there, but definitely not amusement.

'You will be very lucky to avoid criminal proceedings, let alone a lynch party from some of the guests here.'

Truscott was near apoplexy.

'For two pins I would string you up myself were it not for Dr Oakley's remarkably humane attitude to his so-called friends. And I am damned well going to see to it that your unexpected and totally unwelcome arrival here will not upset him any more than is necessary – certainly not his lecture tonight.'

On and on he went (his great fleshy face colouring

steadily, from delicate scarlet to a livid purple) as he told us exactly what he thought of us. We were loathsome, unBritish and beneath contempt; a disgrace to our College and our University and we were in very serious trouble. He, Truscott, would see to that. Our fate now lay in the hands of my former colleague whom we had abandoned without food and water to what might very well have been a horrible end. Why we had returned and how we had managed to wreck a perfectly good boat in the process was quite beyond his comprehension. And it was all due to my academic jealousy of the great concept which Dr Oakley had conceived in the wilderness – the great secret of which was to be revealed that very night to the assembled guests in Dr Oakley's historic lecture.

The arrival of Oakley at the Coral Strand had been a seven-day wonder. He was evidently already a celebrity with the guests: the brilliant scientist who had struggled so courageously to survive and had miraculously returned with a great theory still fresh in his mind. It was as though Charles Darwin had walked from the pages of Joseph Conrad. Even in my shocked and debilitated state I could see the romantic attraction of it to Truscott's prep-school mentality and, at the same time, shuddered at the prospect of what the College Council would make of it all. There was nothing in the College Statutes that dealt with academic piracy and attempted murder on the South Seas. It would, I suppose, all be covered by 'disgraceful conduct' by a Fellow of the College. That would mean calling in the Visitor. I quailed anew at the prospect of explaining all this to the Bishop of Lincoln, as Truscott's anger surged over us like the tidal wave that had taken back the Mara.

Then I became conscious that the diatribe was faltering (largely due to the severe strain to which Truscott had subjected his vocal cords) and that Doris was performing a sort of indignant descant which had previously been drowned by the sheer volume of his rage.

'. . . so you ask the asshole about the canned beef *and* the turtle eggs, if it comes to that – the *asshole* . . .'

Truscott trained his monocle on the small, ragged figure hopping about under his bulbous, sun-burnt nose.

'Madam, I am not going to bandy words with you about the sordid details of this sad affair AND CERTAINLY NOT IN SUCH OBSCENE TERMS.'

This was Truscott's terminal bellow. Perhaps he had damaged his voice permanently.

'Take them away,' he croaked, waving a huge hairy hand in the direction of the sliding door.

We were marched off by the magnificent man in the skirt and the security guard.

Doris disputed every inch of the way, causing a sensation among the colourfully-clad golfers who were propping up the Somerset Maugham Bar. The security guard held Doris firmly by the left arm and propelled her rapidly past the interested gaze of the receptionist who was making a telephone call from the stern of the war canoe.

De Freville and I went quietly, limping after them.

It was a glorious evening. Feathery palm fronds, a hundred feet above our heads, were black and sharply etched against the darkening sky. We slowly plodded towards a low white building which I could just make out in the sunset gloom. It was close to a mangrove shore, next to a tall chain-link fence which, we later discovered, delimited the small area of the Nature Reserve to which the public were admitted.

The thought of Miranda brought a lump to my throat. That formidable young lady now seemed possessed of all the gentle kindness of her desert island prototype. How considerate she had been, despite the ecological enormities that we had committed in her precious sanctuary. I remember wondering if they had abolished capital punishment in Manabau and whether the High Commission would find a lawyer for us. Things would look bad for us if Miranda was called as a witness; we had not even mentioned that Oakley had been on the island. Thank God De Freville was with us. At least his hallowed name might protect us from the full rigours of the law, and from whatever Oakley had in mind. It was surprising that the argumentative De Freville had not put up more of a fight for us. I really thought that he would have made a better lawyer than a historian.

The building towards which we were heading turned out to be a sort of sick-bay or miniature hospital for the various hotels on the bay. Our captors led us through glass swing-doors and switched on some lights to reveal a cool, white-painted corridor. There were pale-green doors to left and right. The security guard fished out a huge bunch of keys and opened the double doors, straight ahead, which led into what seemed to be a small medical ward. There were six beds, three on each side of a long white room, with neatly tucked scarlet blankets and pale-grey curtains that could be drawn for greater privacy. A long scrubbed table stood in the centre of the room with stacked travel magazines and some tattered copies of *Vogue* and *Harper's Bazaar*. There was a door in one corner, which, we soon learned, led to a bathroom and lavatory. There were no proper windows – only long narrow glass slits, well above head height, to illuminate the room during the day. It was deliciously cool from the air-conditioning which, I assumed, was the cause of the faint hum of machinery that I could just detect.

Our filthy gear had already been stacked on the far side of the table. I noticed that they had dumped even the tents and our few dirty cooking utensils. There was, however, no sign of the axe.

The security guard spoke to us for the first time before shutting the door.

'Food should be here for you in half an hour.'

With that he slammed the door. I heard once again a metallic rattling and turning of a key in a lock.

It seemed strange to sit in electric light after weeks of night-time darkness. Everything was so white and clean, apart from us and our belongings.

'Well, I'm going to use the can and then have a shower. *That*, at least, I shall enjoy.'

Doris was evidently recovering from the indignities to which she had been so recently subjected.

De Freville and I discussed the recent terrifying turn of events.

It was quite clear, De Freville reasoned, why Oakley had done what he had. By whatever means he had got round to this side of the island, things would have looked pretty bad for him if our corpses had been later discoverd on the island. And they would look even worse if we turned up alive and kicking and then let on about what had really happened. So, the most sensible course for Oakley to adopt was to claim that he had been marooned by us. This gave him his alibi. If our bodies were later discovered then, as De Freville said: 'Dead men tell no tales.' All this ridiculous business about my academic jealousy would provide the motive for thus disposing of him by stranding him on the island. It would also give him something to show off about when he got back to civilization.

'It might even make the Sunday newspapers,' De Freville concluded. 'I can see the headline now: "Shipwrecked Don's Discovery". It really destroys one's faith in academic respectability.'

Supper was brought to us by another, more friendly security guard while Doris was still in the bathroom. De Freville and I were so hungry that we set to there and then on a gorgeous meal of prawn cocktail, Chicken Supreme Manau and pineapple and ice cream, followed by biscuits and cheese with coffee.

Doris emerged while we were eating dessert, cursing us for not having waited. She was wrapped in an enormous bath towel and looked pristine and flushed with her long black hair falling on her shoulders, as she minutely examined the depleted tray, to make sure that we had not exceeded our alloted portions – which we had not – all the while complaining.

'Jesus, do you guys stink.'

Despite our predicament, I enjoyed that shower more than any other in my life. Bed that night was sheer delight, with the cool cleanness of freshly-laundered sheets in grey-curtained privacy.

Doris was asleep almost as soon as De Freville had switched off the lights, but I lay on my back listening to the faint hum of the air-conditioning with the pleasant knowledge that Doris still had half a sheet of tissue paper hidden away in her rucksack.

20

We slept late on the first morning of captivity and were still in bed when our breakfasts were brought to us by the nasty security guard. He did not speak, but marched in, after much jangling of keys, banged down the tray on the table and stalked out, locking the doors behind him.

He returned half an hour later. This time his arrival was signalled not only by the customary jangling, but by a dull clang and a stealthy scraping as though of wood on concrete. He entered bearing a bucket, complete with cloth and scrubbing brush, a broom and a dust pan.

'You can stuff that lot,' Doris said from the safety of her bed where she was propped up on a bolus of tangled bedclothes, with her curtain pulled back for the day.

'Please yourself, Miss, but you won't get any lunch until this place is cleaned up. You've made it into a proper pig-sty.'

It took De Freville and me the best part of an hour to sweep, scrub and generally tidy up. Doris relented to the extent of making her own bed, which she did very badly.

Then the full implications of our captivity came to me. Strangely, I missed the movement of fresh air on my skin and even the burning sun from which I had so often cringed. The cool antiseptic atmosphere emphasized the feeling of claustrophobia. I dragged up a chair and stood on it to gaze through the narrow horizontal window at the cloud-shrouded mountain from where we had looked down with such foolish hopes on what was now our prison. Had we really found Yeo's Whistling Duck up there *and* De Freville's Petrel? For how much longer would that awful burial place and those strange steps remain hidden by tangled vegetation and swirling mists?

I moved the chair to the other wall, to peer out at the mangroves which were only about fifty yards from our window. There was no sign of holiday-makers, only a Mangrove Heron in stealthy pursuit of fishy prey. I clambered down, carefully brushing off the impression of my shoes from the seat and walked over to Doris. She was again sprawled on her now untidy bed reading the December edition of *Vogue*.

'Doris,' I said, in wheedling tones. 'Would you – could you – see your way to parting with your last piece of tissue paper?'

She flung down the magazine and stared at me with dark belligerent eyes.

'What *is* it with you two?'

'We just wanted to give you a surprise.'

'OK, OK. Help yourselves.'

Doris had drawn the curtain around her bed when De Freville and I emerged from the bathroom. I wrapped the last precious piece of tissue paper around my comb. De Freville leaned forward expectantly, nodded and we were off with 'Surabaya Johnnie'. He got the pitch *exactly*; my modest accompaniment was very much in the spirit of Kurt Weill's conception.

So it was that we recreated the art of Lotte Lenya and the decadence of Berlin in the 1930s in the unlikely surroundings of a bare hotel sick-bay on a remote Pacific island.

Our programme had been carefully chosen during all those clandestine rehearsals in the mangroves, but none of the songs achieved the nostalgic, acid beauty of 'Surabaya

203

Johnnie' – primarily because my tissue paper was becoming soggy and, possibly, because, so long after our last rehearsal, De Freville's voice was distinctly strained by the effort of achieving Lenya's unique timbre.

Doris's head had appeared abruptly from between the curtains at the first languorous notes of 'Surabaya Johnnie' and remained there until we finished. Then she clapped.

'So *that* was the big surprise?'

We nodded.

'I still don't see the connection with bird droppings . . . but it was a great show. Really great.'

Oddly, Doris's expression seemed to contain more relief than musical appreciation. It turned out that she had never heard of Lenya, let along Brecht and Weill, and had no idea why De Freville was singing in such a 'screwy way'. But as Oscar Wilde said, art expresses nothing but itself.

Lunch was brought by the friendly security guard, a tubby New Zealander with a harelip, who apparently had taken up his present employment after a 'spot of trouble at a chicken farm near Auckland'. He told us that his boss (the nasty guard) was helping to organize a sports competition that afternoon. It appeared that the hotels competed, each fortnight, for a sports trophy that remained with the winning establishment until the next contest. The Coral Strand invariably came last in the competition (apart from the golf tournament) owing to the general decrepitude of its more wealthy clientele.

Our gaoler, Harry, told us that Dr Oakley's lecture had, by all accounts, been extremely well attended. Even guests from the 18-30's Club at the other end of the bay had gatecrashed. Harry had not attended. He had been on duty and, in any case, would have preferred to watch a video of a James Bond film in the lounge of the Beachcomber. However, he had heard some of the guests complaining afterwards about the tedium of Oakley's exposition; an elderly American lady had said it was downright disgusting and some of the British guests were going on about squandering the tax-payer's money. Truscott had been more than put out by the topic of the lecture and afterwards had been rude to Oakley in the Somerset Maugham Bar.

This news cheered us considerably: it would at least make it more difficult for Oakley to sustain his absurd story about our having abandoned him because of my jealousy for his brilliant theory.

Harry chatted away with us until we had finished our meal. He took some of our dirty clothes to get them laundered and also fished out an unused draught board and a pack of playing cards from the table drawer before bustling out and locking the double doors at the end of our antiseptic prison. But the afternoon dragged heavily. For much of the time I just stood on a chair gazing up at the mysterious mountain wondering what lingering taboos still protected those strange archaeological remains. I imagined them pitching struggling adulterers from the stone platform. I would have hated to go over the edge with Muriel Oakley. Perhaps there was an ossuary under the fifteenth green.

Doris joined me at the window, then moved to the other one, as I continued my trance-like reverie in the silence of the sunless room.

'*Jesus!*'

Doris's shout nearly made me fall off my chair.

'It's him – the *asshole*. He's out there, as bold as brass. He can't know we're in here.'

205

De Freville and I were at Doris's side in a flash.

There, sure enough, was Oakley pottering about in the dappled shade of the mangroves. He was wearing only scarlet bathing shorts. His head was bent forward as he examined the surface of the swirling brown water.

'My *God*. What wouldn't I give to get out there and give him a piece of my mind.' Doris was jibbering with rage.

'I'm going to do just that,' De Freville muttered as he jumped down and began rummaging about in his rucksack.

I was riveted to the window. Oakley was now squatting in the mangroves still intent on the water surface. As I watched, my hatred subsided to sick despair.

I climbed down and slumped on to my bed, close to tears at the futility of all that had happened since we had been on the island. What could have been so glorious was sullied and destroyed.

De Freville was now kneeling at the double doors, poking with a length of stout wire into the keyhole.

'I always carry this with me, locks are one of my hobbies,' De Freville explained. 'You had better put on you bathing trunks while I'm getting this door open – there could be quite a chase through the mangroves before we catch up with Dr Oakley.'

'Do you mean that you could have got us out of this damned hole *before*?' Doris whispered indignantly, still at the vantage point from which she continued to observe closely the antics of my former colleague.

'Yes, of course. I can open locks. It's like the search for a limited truth. But what would have been the point? We couldn't get off the island by ourselves. All I want now is to reason with Dr Oakley. If we can't persuade him to tell the truth then at least I can give him a piece of my mind.'

De Freville jabbed away at the dark recesses of the lock, while Doris (who had jumped down from her perch) and I changed into bathing gear behind our drawn bed curtains.

It took De Freville about five minutes to pick that lock. When he had opened the door, Doris and I crept along the corridor and peered cautiously out at the hot sunny landscape while De Freville donned his bathing trunks. We could not see Oakley (the mangroves were on the other side of the building) and there was not a soul in sight, only a group of mynah birds squabbling on the dry dusty grass which swept away to an empty coral shore. In the distance I could hear desultory shouts and subdued cheering from the sports gala.

De Freville padded up the corridor behind us, and pushed past into the glaring heat. We followed him round the corner of the sick-bay. My eyes were dazzled by the brilliant sunlight reflected from the white walls of the building.

Oakley was only some seventy yards away, still crouching in the mangrove gloom, a narrow shaft of sunlight catching his gingery hair. We padded silently towards him, a half-naked spearhead with Doris in front and De Freville and me to left and right.

Doris reached the mangroves first. Oakley half-turned his head at the splash of her feet in the water. She thrust at his freckly back with opened hands. Oakley gave a low gasp. He was still toppling forward when De Freville and I got to him a fraction of a second later. De Freville shoved Oakley's head downwards into the muddy water; I put my right foot on to a threshing thigh, which felt soft and fleshy against the hardness of my sole. There was a strong dank smell of decaying mud.

We were all shouting. What exactly I cannot now recall. It all happened so swiftly, that brief surge of hatred at the mangrove edge.

Oakley had been looking at some curious little insects that were skating about in tight formation on the water surface like an armada of tiny aquatic war machines. There were hundreds of them. They too became involved in the mêlée, dashing wildly about, their shiny bodies flashing alternately black and silvery in the broken light.

By the time we stood up, the insects had reformed into a perfectly circular flotilla, shimmering in their constant skating movements in a patch of brilliant sunlight some yards to our right, and Oakley's body was lying, face downwards and motionless, in murky lapping water.

We ran straight back to the sick-bay after murdering Oakley. De Freville came last. He had towed the body away from the mangroves, into deeper water. From the corner of the sick-bay, I looked back to see my former colleague still floating face downwards, already moving gently away from the shore, caught in the tidal race that swept between the mangroves and a long rocky islet which I had not noticed before.

De Freville relocked our door while Doris showered herself in the bathroom. I stood on the chair to glimpse the scarlet smudge of Oakley's bathing trunks drift beyond my angle of vision from the narrow window.

21

We never spoke about the drowning of Oakley: not on the island or afterwards. We had gone down to the mangroves simply to reason with him or, at the very worst, 'to give him a piece of our minds' (as De Freville had put it). Yet with a single concerted impulse we had forced the poor fellow down into the muddy sea water and held him there for what must have been several minutes, cursing and shouting obscenities all the while.

The extraordinary thing is how I managed to bear such appalling guilt. But strangely I did not feel an evil man.

De Freville and Doris must have been as devastated as I was. Yet they gave few signs of it, except that they were both silent and very subdued immediately after the terrible goings-on in the mangroves. Doris retired to the bathroom as soon as we got back to the sick-bay and stayed there for at least an hour. Once I thought I heard faint sobbing sounds coming through the door. After relocking our prison De Freville got on to his bed and drew the curtains. I returned to my station at the window to gaze again at the misty mountainside.

Harry returned later in the afternoon, bearing tea, Osborne biscuits and the tidings that the 18-30's Club had again triumphed in the sports gala and that the Coral Strand lot, such was their decrepitude, had failed again, *even in the golf tournament*. In our gaoler's opinion, the regular defeat of the swankiest establishment on the island was a great embarrassment to Mr Truscott, who was under considerable pressure to abandon the event.

Oakley's corpse was found the following morning. The discovery was revealed to us by Truscott himself. He arrived in an agitated state, accompanied by the nasty security guard, who seemed to be vaguely amused by the latest turn of events.

It appeared that poor Oakley's body had been spotted by an early-morning sail-board enthusiast at the other end of the bay. Although my former colleague was in a very bloated state, and much of his abdomen missing, there was no doubt as to his identity. There was also no question in Truscott's mind as to the cause of death. Sharks. That was what was upsetting him. It was, apparently, the third such fatality in the past two months on what had been widely advertised as an entirely shark-free stretch of water.

I could sympathize with Truscott's feelings, for, as I explained to him, I too had been considerably put out by the loss of an undergraduate in north Cornwall only two years previously. Truscott ignored this friendly overture.

However, his attitude seemed to have changed dramatically since our last encounter. There was now no possibility of bringing charges against us. Instead, he seemed to want us off the island at the earliest opportunity. Having learned of the scientific objectives of Oakley's expedition he now entertained doubts about our sanity.

'A damned queer business altogether and a damned queer bunch mixed up in it. It's more than I can cope with, what with all I've got on my plate, I can tell you . . .'

I suspected that the matter of the sports gala was also bearing heavily on Truscott that morning. He still kept us under lock and key, little realizing my undergraduate's facility with a piece of wire. Nor that I wanted anyone to know about *that*.

210

Truscott bustled in and out three times that day. At each appearance he seemed more harassed. His left eye became increasingly bloodshot and he experienced difficulty in retaining his monocle in place.

On his second visit, which swiftly followed the first, he told us of his problems: of how 'things' did not last long in the tropics and how unco-operative were the kitchen managers of the Coral Strand and the Beachcomber in what they would and would not admit to their cold-room and freezer. But he had sorted out that one – Oakley's mangled body was to be flown out that day, by sea plane, to Manau. There would be an autopsy and a swift cremation. I was to draft a message to the College, which I did there and then ('Regret Derek Oakley passed away in marine mishap. We are safe. Will return asap. Yeo').

I quaked at the thought of poor Muriel Oakley learning of that message – probably from Cecil Fox. It was not only the pain that it would cause her, there was a curious lingering shame for that incident on poor Oakley's Parker Knoll.

On his third visit, Truscott revealed how we were to be got 'off his plate'. We were to leave by the hydrofoil for Manau next morning. There we would be met by someone from the High Commission who would complete the arrangements for our return to the UK. They would even cable our flight number to the College.

Thus it was that we left Ru-in, the tropical paradox into which we had so innocently sailed all those weeks before in pursuit of the ultimate truth of the insect rectum. For the third time, the mountain top was clear, its squat summit golden and brown in brilliant sunshine and dissected with jagged purplish shadows, as wispy clouds crept across its northern slopes to veil the wonders of which we could never speak.

211

'Jesus, to think we climbed that sonofabitch,' Doris said, as she dumped her rucksack beside me on the orange plastic seat of the hydrofoil.

She was inaccurate, as usual. We had only clambered over the western shoulder.

I decided to keep Oakley's ashes in my hand luggage. Pearce-Goodenough, the man from the High Commission, gave me the urn as we drove to Manau International Airport. It was not really an urn – more like a tall Wedgwood sugar bowl. I suppose that it was the best they could find at such short notice. The trouble was that the metal lid was badly fitting and I was worried that the contents might spill into my toilet things. Doris found some Elastoplasts in the remnants of our first-aid kit which served well enough, and I put the thing in the plastic carrier bag that they gave me when I bought some perfume for Molly in the duty-free shop.

There were no real problems on the return flight except at Nadi airport where a bossy official caught me testing the Elastoplast seals *after* we had passed through the security check. I reassured him with the certificate which I had been given at the High Commission. Unfortunately, I refitted the lid rather lopsidedly and was agitated to find that the contents seemed somewhat depleted when I replaced the Elastoplast in the crowded transit lounge at Honolulu. It may, of course, have been that they had settled in the pot, for I could find no evidence of spillage.

We were all very tired on the last lap of the flight to Heathrow. Nevertheless, Doris insisted that we co-ordinate our versions of the events on the island as the 747 circled over the Berkshire countryside.

'We were shipwrecked. OK?'

212

De Freville and I nodded as the no smoking signs pinged on.

'We lost contact with the . . . the other member of the party . . . after the tidal wave. OK? And we never went up on to the mountain or any of that stuff. We promised. Right?'

'OK.'

'And *then* we found our way round to the tourist section *after* he got there . . . OK?'

We nodded again.

'And that shark business happened while we were locked up in the sick-bay. OK?'

'I wonder how he got round to the other side?' De Freville mused above the steady whine and whooshing of air as Staines reservoir slid into view below.

22

There was a message for me at the airport. De Freville spotted it in the thicket of envelopes and folded papers pinned to a noticeboard near the UK and Commonwealth passport control. It was a pencilled note, scrawled on pale-blue paper roughly torn from its pad leaving the words *the caring airline* at the top of the page. 'Telephone message received at 5.10 P.M.' it was headed in spidery writing and then, in rough block capitals: 'MEETING THE 20.35 AND 22.05 TRAINS FROM L'POOL ST – WILL EXPLAIN – FOX'.

'That's extremely thoughful of Dr Fox,' De Freville said.

'Yes, but what's he got to *explain*?'

As far as I could see, it would be I who had to do the explaining, especially about the bulging yellow plastic carrier bag with the magenta lettering: 'THE LAST WORD IN DUTY-FREE – *from Manau International Airport*'.

We parted company on the underground train. De Freville got off at Earls Court, *en route* for Paddington and north Gloucestershire; Doris alighted at Knightsbridge to stay with an elder sister (who was living somewhere off the Brompton Road) before returning to New Jersey.

I could not bear to look at them as they said goodbye.

The carriage emptied at Green Park. I suppose it was about half-past seven of what must have been a pleasant, late-summer day. The slatted wooden floor was strewn with dirty litter. I remembered the high mountain slopes, hidden by mists and trees, where we had eaten lizards and whistling ducks and clawed our way upwards in steaming heat to feel the cool sea breeze on our faces. For the first time in years I had lived, fully and intensely, only to blunder into Truscott's tourist nightmare and that appalling fracas in the mangroves.

The train slowed into another bare neon-lit station. It looked abandoned, scruffy and hopeless – almost derelict. A score or so of passengers were straggled in twos and threes down the platform. The carriage doors hissed and jerked apart. There was a waft of stale air and, behind me, footsteps, a woman's voice and then a man's, high-pitched and querulous.

'The food was really too appalling . . .'

'And the '82 Cissac had absolutely no finish to it.'

The 8.35 was waiting at platform 7 when I arrived, twenty minutes early, at Liverpool Street. I tried to phone Molly, as I had from Heathrow, but there was no answer. My shabby jeans and rucksack made me feel like an elderly teenager as I trudged the length of the train to find a carriage with separate compartments: I intended stretching out on a seat, for I was jet-lagged, dreadfully tired and missing Doris and De Freville desperately. I had never experienced such loneliness before.

Eight weeks earlier, I would as soon have cut my throat as lie like a down-and-out on the seat of a railway compartment. Invariably, summer or winter, I sat bolt upright in what Molly called my 'London suit' – ten years old, discreetly grey, the trousers slightly bell-bottomed – reading or rereading the *Spectator*. Now I was beyond caring, sprawled out with the dusty smell of the green upholstery in my nostrils. Was this the mysterious uncut moquette they spoke of in furniture advertisements? I had always been fascinated by this. What was it that was uncut? What was the difference if it *was* cut? I'll bet it wasn't the stuff on Muriel Oakley's sofa.

I dozed with these questions revolving stupidly in my mind. But only briefly, for I was jolted awake by the sliding thud of the door and a young woman's voice, shrill and excited.

'Yeah, they're a terrific group – really ace . . .' she faltered; then I heard the door slide again. 'There's some old bloke laid out in there,' she said to a companion, who from his grunting seemed to be male.

The door clicked; the voices faded; I remained motionless with my eyes closed.

There were more voices, distant and close, and footsteps and occasional clattering noises echoing from somewhere far outside. No one else came to the compartment until the train juddered very slightly and began slowly to move forward. There were footsteps in the corridor and the door was flung open with a crash. Someone entered the compartment. I opened my eyes and swung into a sitting position to find myself looking straight at the reptilian face of Simms, the University Reader in Agricultural Ergonomics.

'Hello, Reg,' I croaked. It was the only time I had ever called him by his first name. I was still upset after parting from Doris and De Freville.

'Good evening, Yeo,' he replied, his grating voice rising slightly in surprise.

He carefully placed his briefcase on the seat, opened it and took out a pile of neatly stacked papers.

'These government research cuts. Will they never end?'

I grunted as if in sympathy.

Simms droned on about the meeting of some government organization or other that he had just attended ('and which *should* have finished at five-thirty'). There was evidently a severe shortage of money for research and much acrimony about the way it was apportioned. On and on he went, about which committee should have done this and what Under-Secretary should have done that to preserve the future of British agricultural ergonomics. I didn't know what ergonomics were and diverted myself by thinking of the poor leatherback that Simms so startlingly resembled – except for the vertical eyeslits. The skin of her belly had been soft and velvety.

Eventually my companion fell silent. It was not until the train was pulling into Cambridge station that Simms addressed me again.

'Forgive my preoccupation, Yeo. Very remiss of me. I forgot to ask you – have you had a good holiday?'

'Middling,' I replied.

'Excellent, excellent . . . Good gracious, there's Fox waiting on the platform. I thought he never travelled by train. Must get along. And you must tell me about your holiday some time . . .'

Simms made a surprisingly athletic leap on to the platform and dashed for the exit, barely slowing to nod at Fox while I dumped my rucksack on the platform.

'Come along, Yeo. Let me, at it were, help you with your things.'

The familiar tones were as smooth as ever, but there was none of the amused malice with which he usually regarded me. Before I could reply, Fox also legged it to the exit, taking the duty-free bag and the canvas grip. I puffed after him, the rucksack slung uncomfortably across my right shoulder.

'Fox, for God's sake! Be careful with the duty-free bag.'

He was waiting for me outside the station. It was dark

now. Rain was falling gently in weird neon light. Fox had dumped my belongings on the pavement.

Then, again, he was running away.

'I'll fetch my car from the car park,' he shouted over his shoulder. 'Stay here, Yeo – then you won't get wet.'

He disappeared rapidly into the gloom. There was no sign of Simms. A party of excited Japanese teenagers was jostling and jockeying for position at a line of wet, empty taxis. It was the first rain that I had felt on my face since we slept by the dark lake and I had hungered for stewed lizard.

It took five minutes for Fox to glide up in his ancient maroon-coloured Daimler. I noticed that one of the side-lights was not working. His furrowed face was a greyish-white slab, blurred by the streaming windscreen.

A window whirred down,

'Hop in, old chap. Put your stuff in the back.'

I clambered wearily in beside Fox, cradling the duty-free bag.

'I don't suppose you feel up to talking about poor Oakley just at this moment. What a ghastly business it must have been for you. I feel quite responsible, having brought you all together, as it were.'

He paused and shot me a sidelong glance, before carefully overtaking two cyclists wobbling along in the teeming rain. I guessed what was on his mind: after a discreet interval there would be more sly jokes at my expense with his cronies ('to lose an undergraduate would have been *unfortunate* but to lose a Fellow is downright *careless*'. Christ!).

'The undergraduates are all right, I suppose?'

I nodded in the half-light.

'Again, I feel some responsibility for foisting Miss Lakowski on you – and De Freville, of course. Her father

218

wanted her out of the way, you know, that's why I added her to the party. Funny business altogether. But it was a good opportunity. Old Lakowski is as rich as Croesus and . . . well, it seemed a good idea at the time and there might have been a benefaction.'

I'll bet there might have been. How much did Fox get out of it, I wondered?

'A fishy business,' Fox mused. 'It seems that old Lakowski is in trouble in the States at the moment. Tax evasion, possible Mafia connection – all that sort of thing. The Master is quite worried about the tie-up with Kramer College. Thinks it could be a way of laundering money. Still, I mustn't bother you with all that business.'

'No,' I agreed. 'But why are we going *this* way?'

'I thought we could have a drink in College. Give you a chance to sort yourself out, as it were.'

'But I want to go home.'

'Yes . . . we can talk about that, too.'

'What do you mean, talk about it? Now look, it's very kind of you and all that . . .'

'Think nothing of it, my dear fellow – least I can do under the circumstances.'

'Well, you've been very kind and especially to leave that message at Heathrow. I didn't know you could do that. But what is it that you want to explain?'

'Explain?'

Fox shifted uneasily on his comfortably padded leather seat.

'Yes, in your message you said "will explain".'

'Oh, *that*. You'll see soon enough.'

'Now look here, Fox. I've had enough surprises to last me . . .'

'Yes, I know. This has been a damnably unfortunate business. But there's something I must tell you.'

'But . . .'

'No! I insist. You mustn't upset yourself unnecessarily, my dear Yeo. Now please leave me to concentrate on driving, I can hardly *see* through the windscreen it's coming down so fast.'

Fox drove grimly along the empty road which glistened in the yellow glow of the street lights.

'I'll pour you a stiff drink and you'll soon be as right as rain,' Fox said as we turned into the College gates.

The lights were full on in the empty Porter's lodge.

Fox drove slowly into the Fellows' car park and deftly brought the vehicle to a halt exactly between adjacent, parallel white lines. He switched off the engine, released his seat belt and reached across to open my door.

'Leave your things in the car. No need to lug them about in all this rain. Just go across to my room.'

Although he paused to lock the car, my plump colleague overtook me at a steady trot as I stumbled through the torrential gloom (still clutching my yellow duty-free bag). He was waiting for me at the bottom of H Staircase, which evidently still lacked a light bulb.

I could see a strip of light beneath Fox's door as we groped our way up the dark stairs.

Fox took off his coat, shook it and flung open the door, as though about to reveal a carefully prepared surprise. Had he got Molly in there? I wanted to see her so much.

But there was no one there. Just the familiar Foxian elegance, exactly as I remembered it: the ormolu and veneered tulipwood *tables ambulantes*, which Fox had somehow acquired during the early years of his Fellowship; a tasteful scattering of ivory figures on the mantelshelf; the scarlet doctoral gown carefully folded across the back of a chintz-covered wing chair. A half-finished *petit point* embroidery, apparently of naked nymphs, lay on one of the *tables*.

'Will you have sherry – or something stronger?'

'Whisky, thank you, Fox.'

'I've got Glenfiddich. Kept it for poor Oakley when he used to drop in for a chat.' Fox paused to replace the bottle, thoughtfully stroking the luxuriant nostril hair with his left hand. 'Oh dear, what a sad business this has turned out to be.'

He handed me my whisky, then fiddled with a wine glass and thoughtfully drew the silver-capped cork from a blue, Bristol glass decanter.

I caught his eye and glimpsed for a split second such a glitter of malign satisfaction that I nearly spilled my drink.

'You may have guessed, Yeo, why I've brought you here.'

Fox's epiglottis shot up convulsively as he sipped his sherry. It remained out of sight for several seconds and then cautiously reappeared as he swallowed. We were both still standing; he had not invited me to sit.

'Muriel,' he announced theatrically, lingering over the '*l*' to give a faintly French flavour.

'Muriel Oakley? What about her?'

'You must appreciate that in the present tragic circumstances and in view of what, as it were . . . went on between you it puts her in a very difficult position.'

'Now look here, Fox . . .'

'My dear Yeo, there is no need to be embarrassed or to beat about the bush for that matter. These things happen. All too frequently, I'm afraid.'

Fox paused, sipped delicately at his sherry and leaned forward, his voice dropping to a whisper that made my flesh creep.

'But it *is* awkward. You see, Muriel told me about

221

your . . . ah . . . attempt on her. I must say, you didn't waste much time. Poor Oakley was hardly airborne apparently . . .'

'Now look here, Fox . . .'

'No, no. Hear me out. There is absolutely no point in upsetting yourself, Yeo. It's all over and done with. Muriel and I agreed on that.'

'Muriel and *you*?' I was entirely lost. Fox sailed on, apparently unaware of the interruption.

'She is a very remarkable woman. We've been very good friends for – oh – more than six years now. All quite discreet, of course, but Muriel has come to depend on me more and more, especially since you left for your Pacific jaunt. She has been exceptionally brave, but is feeling very vulnerable and is worried that you might . . . well . . . be over-anxious to comfort her now that she's on her own. That's why I have, as it were, inveigled you here and because, as I have said, I do feel a *certain* responsibility.' His eyes flashed briefly. 'After all, it was my idea for you to go along with the Lakowski girl and young De Freville.'

'The Lakowski girl'! Muriel Oakley had used those very words when she had appeared by the waterfall. I had certainly never heard anyone speak about Doris in that way. Muriel said that Fox had added Doris because she was 'dangerous' and that De Freville was 'potty'. I suppose that I was his last fatal ingredient.

He droned on, but I didn't listen. My legs were aching; I was almost prostrate with weariness. And I wanted so much to see Molly. Her face appeared to me through waves of fatigue: corn-coloured hair, faintly flecked with white, curling on the neck; her nose tipped up at the end; the dimple which was deeper on the left cheek – a quizzical smile flickering round her lips.

222

Fox was sitting down now, going on about taking Muriel to meet his old mother in Dorking. Good God, this was too much! I just had to get out. I would walk through the rain to Molly.

I got up and blundered rudely out of the room, crashing down the stone steps into the wet, lamplit court. I wondered if Fox was still following. Then I realized that I was still clutching the duty-free bag. I turned back up the dark staircase with Oakley's mortal remains swinging from my hand, and plodded towards the thin line of light showing beneath Fox's door.

The door opened almost before I had knocked. I thrust the bag into Fox's hands. It seemed the best thing to do in the circumstances.